S0-ABB-174

Dear Reader,

Amnesia has to be my favorite topic to explore in a story, and *Unforgettable* takes this to the extreme with heroine Erin Riley, a firefighter who has forgotten *everything*—including the man she loved and left. The challenge of writing a character who is essentially a blank slate was a lot of fun, but also I could imagine how frightening it would be to suddenly wake up and not even know your name.

It's certainly no easier to be forgotten—such is the fate of our hero, Bo Myers. Fire investigator Bo is trying to move on after breaking up with Erin, but now she needs his help, and how can he walk away when she needs him?

This couple is one of my favorites (I know, I always say that), because of the challenges that they face and because they prove that in the final analysis, when everything else seems lost, love remains. It's also the first Harlequin Blaze novel I've set in Syracuse, New York, where I live.

If you want to chat about this new Blaze book, please drop me an email at samhunter@samanthahunter.com, or you can find me on Twitter and Facebook.

Good reading!

Sam

Unforgettable

—

Samantha Hunter

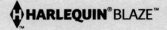

Recycling programs
for this product may
not exist in your area.

ISBN-13: 978-0-373-79783-7

UNFORGETTABLE

Copyright © 2014 by Samantha Hunter

All rights reserved. Except for use in any review, the reproduction or
utilization of this work in whole or in part in any form by any electronic,
mechanical or other means, now known or hereafter invented, including
xerography, photocopying and recording, or in any information storage
or retrieval system, is forbidden without the written permission of the
publisher, Harlequin Enterprises Limited, 225 Duncan Mill Road,
Don Mills, Ontario, Canada M3B 3K9.

This is a work of fiction. Names, characters, places and incidents are
either the product of the author's imagination or are used fictitiously,
and any resemblance to actual persons, living or dead, business
establishments, events or locales is entirely coincidental.

This edition published by arrangement with Harlequin Books S.A.

For questions and comments about the quality of this book,
please contact us at CustomerService@Harlequin.com.

® and TM are trademarks of Harlequin Enterprises Limited or its
corporate affiliates. Trademarks indicated with ® are registered in the
United States Patent and Trademark Office, the Canadian Trade Marks
Office and in other countries.

Printed in U.S.A.

ABOUT THE AUTHOR

Samantha Hunter lives in Syracuse, New York, where she writes full-time for Harlequin. When she's not plotting her next story, Sam likes to work in her garden, quilt, cook, read and spend time with her husband and their dogs. Most days you can find Sam chatting on the Harlequin Blaze boards at Harlequin.com, or you can check out what's new, enter contests or drop her a note at her website, www.samanthahunter.com.

Books by Samantha Hunter

HARLEQUIN BLAZE

*The HotWires
**American Heroes
†The Berringers

To get the inside scoop on Harlequin Blaze and its talented writers, be sure to check out blazeauthors.com.

Other titles by this author available in ebook format.

For Sandy, always a puppy in my heart.

1

"Erin, c'mon, you'll have fun, and if anyone needs to have some fun, it's you."

Erin Riley shook her head at her friend Dana Rogers, who grabbed Erin's hand and pulled.

"Come join me," Dana invited. "Let loose."

Erin let her friend drag her along, and before she knew it, strong arms were boosting them up on top of the bar. Dana was grinning like the wild woman that she was, dancing even before the music started.

They were having a fun night out, and as she looked around the bar, Erin was self-conscious at first. She seriously thought about climbing back down, but everyone was watching and chanting *dance, dance, dance*.

So she started to dance, and that's when things got better. A lot better.

Letting go, she raised her arms high and put more hip-swing into it, much to the crowd's appreciation. Dana hooted in approval and danced with her. Erin had to admit, she enjoyed how the guys were slack-jawed as they watched. She smiled at them and winked as she turned and shimmied to a blaring version of "I'm

Alright." For that one moment, she *was* all right. Perfect, in fact.

Erin felt sexy, which she hadn't in a long time.

Noting the heat in the eyes of a few men who watched, she also felt powerful. In control, for the first time in a while.

Dana was right. This was exactly what Erin needed, so she planned to enjoy herself. This was her second chance. She wasn't going to waste one single minute.

She'd almost died, after all. A former firefighter, she'd been inside a building when an explosion had knocked her down and she'd been trapped by a loose beam. After several brain surgeries and a week in an induced coma, she'd come out of it all with no memory of her life. Most of her adult past had been obliterated, though she could remember her childhood. The doctors said it was uncertain when or how much of her memory would come back.

Tastes and some emotions remained. She could like or dislike something—a place, food, etc. She could experience familiarity, without remembering something exactly. It was the same with people. For instance, the firemen she'd worked with for eight years had been her support system since she got out of the hospital. Still, they were strangers to her—mostly. When she was with them, or with Dana or her sister, she could *feel* the familiarity even when she couldn't remember their history together.

She couldn't, however, recall anything about the accident or being a firefighter. Another member of her crew had died in the same incident, and there was an ongoing investigation since the fire had been arson.

Erin couldn't remember what happened. And she

had tried. She had suffered and punished herself for not being able to remember, and she couldn't do it anymore. All she knew was what people told her.

She also couldn't remember who she was, but she finally realized that meant she could be anyone she wanted. Smiling as someone handed her a beer, she and Dana danced right into the next song.

Good thing she'd worn her new jeans and one of those tees that showed a teeny hint of belly. It was all courtesy of a recent shopping trip with Dana, who had helped Erin supplement her otherwise pitiful wardrobe. Apparently it was something Dana had wanted to do for quite some time.

When she'd gotten home from the hospital, Erin thought there must be a guy living at her house. Most of her clothes were for work or bore the insignias of her department. Not a single pair of high heels in the lot—not like the ones she was wearing now.

Even her pajamas were cotton pants and oversize fire department T-shirts.

Those days were over.

Sending a sexy smile to the cute bartender, she planned on making up for lost time. She tilted her head back and chugged her beer as the song ended, enjoying the chants that accompanied her finale.

When she was done, her head spun. Her skin was warm. She laughed, wobbling a bit as she handed her glass back to the bartender.

She and Dana finally made their way down off the bar to riotous applause. Several burly men—most of them firemen or cops—happily offered a helping hand.

Dana was a dispatcher and engaged to a firefighter

in the unit Erin had worked with. He met her back on the floor with a kiss.

"I can't leave you alone for a minute, can I?" Scott scolded, but he was grinning. His eyes were warm as he took in his fiancée. Erin averted her eyes discreetly from the deepening kiss that the two were sharing in front of everyone.

Erin cleared her throat. "Okay, well, then, I'll just go back to the table and eat all of those wings."

Dana never broke the kiss while waving her away, making Erin laugh. She suspected the lovebirds were going to find some privacy, and she left them to it.

As she walked back to their table, she figured she should have known better. She could hear the boisterous voices of the crew the minute she crossed the floor toward the tables at the back. They saw her, too. No doubt they'd seen her up on the bar, as well.

"What's up, Buttercup?" Hank shouted.

"Tulip!" Leroy followed up.

"Daisy!" Derek added with a snicker.

The last one got a round of high fives as Erin took a breath and approached the group, smirking at them for teasing her about her work at the flower shop. Her sister owned the shop and had taken her on as soon as Erin was able.

Still, it was a far cry from being a firefighter to working as a florist. Not so long ago, she'd been one of the guys, so she tried to act like it. As if nothing had changed.

"You guys calling each other pet names again?" she asked as she joined them. Giving as good as she got was par for the course with this bunch. "Leroy *must* be Daisy, since he's always fresh as one."

Another round of laughter rose and then settled down as Leroy eyed her from the other side of the long table.

"Someday, when your memory comes back, you'll pay for that one." The threat was playful and made with a glint in his eye.

"I hope that day comes," she said, more serious than she meant to be.

"We do, too," Pete said as they all became quiet.

Erin frowned. "Sorry, didn't mean to be a downer. Hand me a beer?"

"Gladly. Nice moves up there, by the way. We never knew you could dance like that."

"Yeah, me, either."

She accepted another beer and helped herself to some wings.

"Carry on, then," she said, waving them on like a queen to her subjects. That succeeded in lightening the mood again.

"Hey, we thought of something that could help with your memory," Leroy said.

"Yeah. What?"

"You said the doctors told you that things from your life before could help bring your memory back, right? We have a lot of stories we could tell."

"Those stories are probably things she'd rather leave forgotten," Pete said with a grin.

Erin smiled. It was good to be around friends who could joke with her about her memory loss. It balanced out the absolute terror and grief that had been frequent, though less so these days.

"I'm game. Take your best shot."

"Well, there was this time when Riley came run-

ning out from that fire at the old folks' home, carrying
the older gentleman, buck naked and thrown over her
shoulder," Pete offered with a wry smile. "They got
him on the gurney and he wouldn't let the medics take
him away until he asked her out on a date."

Erin's jaw dropped. "That did *not* happen."

She liked how they called her by her last name. She
felt more like a "Riley" than an "Erin" anyway, in spite
of her sexy clothes.

"Oh, it really did. And you said yes."

The guys made a few lewd comments and laughter
picked up, and Derek put a hand on her arm.

"You were being kind. You brought him dinner
a couple of nights when he was in the hospital and
watched TV with him. That was your date. He passed
away a few months later, and his family sent you a
thank-you for your visits."

Erin swallowed hard and nodded.

"There was also the time we told you everyone was
dressing up for duty on Halloween and you showed
up at the station as Princess Leia. The alarm rang almost as soon as you arrived. You had to change in the
truck, which you did, without batting an eye, I'll add.
Though you fought the whole fire wearing the braids.
I have to find the picture that made it into the paper,"
Pete said nostalgically.

Even Erin had to laugh at that. She lifted her hand
to her hair, now boy-short as it grew in after being cut
and shaved for surgeries. She couldn't remember it
long, but in most of the pictures she saw, she wore either ponytails or braids. She wasn't sure if she'd grow it
long again. Having it short was convenient, especially

for summer. Her sister said it framed her face better, and made her eyes look bigger.

"You always swore like a sailor. More quarters in the jar for pizza night from you than anyone."

Erin appreciated them filling in gaps for her, but the stories felt as if they were about someone else. She was just getting to know these people whom she had known for years. Men and women who had trusted her with their lives.

She wanted to have it all back, her history with these people. Her whole life. It wasn't likely; the doctors said the longer she didn't recall anything, the less chance that she would.

She put her beer on the table as her eyes burned.

"Hey, you okay?"

"Yeah, fine," she said, pretending to bend to fix the strap on her shoe while she got hold of her emotions.

Apparently, they did this often, getting together for sports or food. Erin couldn't remember, but it did feel normal. Normal was nice.

When she rose, they were already talking about other things—sports and upcoming vacations. She took a chair near the wall and munched on her wings.

As she licked some of the sauce from her fingers, she stopped and looked up, feeling as if she was being watched. And she was.

Bo Myers sat across the room, alone at his table, his eyes glued to her as if she were the only one there. His eyes rooted her to the spot and sent licks of heat scattering over her skin. She lost track of everything and almost tumbled her plate to the floor, catching it before it fell.

He was the local fire marshal. She'd met with him

a few times since the accident. He'd been there when she'd woken up in the hospital.

He was an intense, somewhat intimidating man in every way—tall, brooding and powerful—with a serious face and eyes that meant business. She wasn't sure she'd ever seen him smile. Irrationally, she always wanted to touch his hair. Bristly on top, but soft, she imagined. As if he had just rolled out of bed or gotten caught in a strong wind.

His magnetic eyes were, right now, focused on the finger she had been sucking some of the wing sauce from. She removed it from between her lips and grabbed a napkin.

The guys told her that Bo had been one of their crew before he'd moved on to being an investigator. It was hard to imagine. He was terse, quiet, and not at all like the rest of the group.

There was no question that he affected her differently than the other guys. They were all handsome, fit, and yet she felt nothing but some vague friendliness toward all of them. As if they were her brothers, or at least friends.

Bo, whom she hardly knew at all, had been taking center stage in her dreams lately—in a mostly naked way. The way he was looking at her now was almost as if he were angry, or as if he were undressing her. She wasn't sure which, or which she wanted it to be.

"I think it's time for me to go," she said too brightly. She stood, pushing her plate to the side.

The guys barely noticed, and after a round of good-byes, she decided to walk home. Her house was only a mile away and she needed the fresh air. And to get away from Bo Myers. But as she walked to the door, she made the mistake of looking back. His gaze met hers across the room, sending a shiver down her spine.

Then, as she reached for the door, he got up and headed directly toward her.

Bo wasn't sure why he was following Erin as she left. She didn't want his company. He should definitely keep his distance, as he had been doing. A clear, professional distance that ate away at him a bit each day.

He couldn't remember the last time he'd slept except due to sheer exhaustion. He'd come here tonight to remedy that with a few drinks. Maybe more than a few. He didn't know she'd be here, and if he had, he would have avoided the bar completely. There were plenty more in Syracuse.

He thought he was seeing things when she'd gotten up on that bar—or rather when she'd been hoisted up by a guy with his hands on her ass. Her dancing had nearly killed him. It was so unlike her—except in private. She'd danced for him plenty of times—only for him.

The Erin he'd known would have died before dancing on a bar like that. Dana did it all the time. It was part of her personality, to be wild. Flirtatious. No one took it seriously—if they did, they'd have to deal with Scott.

But Erin, no way. It was all he could do not to drag her down off the bar, but what she did wasn't his business anymore. Unfortunately, his body didn't agree. When she'd started licking the barbecue sauce from her fingers, he'd stiffened and had to wait until he could stand up again.

He'd watched how she laughed and smiled with her

crew, not noticing their covert glances at her curves and movements. She'd been one of them, one of the guys—but not now. They touched her more often than they did before. Casual, supportive touches, but still. Things were already changing.

Bo noticed, because he couldn't touch her at all.

As he caught up with her, she stilled, looking right and left as if seeking an escape. That irritated him. He'd never done anything to hurt her. Quite the opposite.

"Riley," he said, feeling like a teenager who was talking to the beautiful girl he wanted, but he had nothing prepared to say.

He blinked, his head buzzing. Maybe he should have skipped that last Scotch.

"How are you?" he managed to ask.

Erin always had a way of looking at him. Her clear green eyes would darken to a mossy-jade, and she would seem to completely absorb him with that gaze. For a second, he'd caught that look again when their eyes met across the room. Bo felt that connection, strong as ever. He wanted to think what they'd had was too strong for the explosion, or her amnesia, to wipe out.

But now she looked at him like a stranger. There was a gleam of panic in her expression, as well. Why?

"Hello, Marshal. I'm good. Thanks. Actually, um, I was just leaving." Her tone was distant, polite. Eager to go.

She was the woman he knew—in her movements, her expressions—but in many ways she was oddly unfamiliar.

He knew what every inch of her smelled like, tasted

like. He knew everything she liked in bed and out, and the memories of it had haunted him for months. The thought of touching her made his heart slam harder in his chest.

They'd broken up a month before her accident, and in that time, he'd missed her deeply.

What was there to say, really? He'd asked her to make a choice, and she had. It wasn't him. Everything hadn't been right between them, he knew that. They both had secrets, both held back. When he wanted more, she wasn't willing to give it.

That was that.

The day of the explosion was one of the worst moments of his life.

But she was alive. Here in front of him, staring at him as though she very much wanted him to leave her alone.

To her, he was just another jerk in a bar. Or not even that. Anger boiled inside him, not at her, but at the situation. How many times, and in how many ways, could he lose this woman?

"'Night, Marshal." She slipped out the door into the evening without another word.

Bo took a long breath and returned to his table and sat, throwing back the last of the Scotch he'd ordered, cursing under his breath as he tossed a few bills on the table. He told himself to let her walk away.

"Everything okay, Bo?"

It was Hank, one of the crew. Bo had worked with them for five years after leaving the New York State Police, with his eye on the job he had now as an investigator. It was his ultimate goal—the only thing he ever wanted, except for Erin. He had to forget about her, especially when he was investigating her case.

Not that it was getting anywhere. She was the only witness to what had happened, and she couldn't remember a thing. It had been arson, though they had very little evidence to pursue. Whoever had set the fire had known what they were doing. Bo worried that they'd do it again if he couldn't catch them, but he had four other cases waiting on his desk.

"Yeah, everything's fine."

He dismissed Hank, heading for the door. He didn't feel like sitting around making small talk, and he could get drunk in his own living room.

It was a warm June night, and he walked out into the parking lot where the faint smell of cigarette smoke hung in the air. Picnic tables lined a patch of worn grass that ran down the side of the lot, where folks could hang out or smoke. Or find a few minutes alone, away from the crowded bar.

He looked for Erin, hoping she hadn't driven after how much she'd been drinking. He heard a noise, and spotted her at the edge of the lot. She was sitting at one of the tables.

"Erin?"

She turned, startled. "Oh, hi. Again."

"What are you doing?"

He saw her shrug in silhouette. "Just getting some air. Seeing how many constellations I can remember and wondering for the one millionth time why I can tell you exactly where the Big Dipper is but I can't tell you anything really important."

He nodded. "Well, you know the doctors said—"

"I know what they said," she cut him off. "It was more of a rhetorical question."

"Right. Sorry."

"Why are you out here?"

"I was leaving, but I'm glad to catch you before you left. You know, back in the bar...the dancing. That probably wasn't a great idea."

She frowned. "Why not?"

"You might go back to the job, or at least to the department, someday. You don't want to change the way the guys see you, and believe me, they're looking at you differently these days."

She shrugged a second time.

"I don't care. And it's really none of your business."

She'd gotten up from the table, intended to walk past him. He caught her arm gently, stopping her. He left it there for a beat, then dropped his hold.

"There's something else."

"What?"

"Joe's family. They want you investigated. Including any past reports or problems."

"Why?"

"They're grieving, looking for explanations."

"So they think they can pin his death on me?"

"They can't, and their accusations are unfounded, we know that. But it would be advisable to keep, well, a lower profile, I suppose. Until things are settled."

Now he was talking stupid, too. It was the truth about Joe's family, but none of this would impact the investigation. They had no grounds, medical or otherwise, to think that Erin was at fault.

Bo was telling her what he needed to tell her. For his

own reasons. It might not be right, but that was something different altogether.

"Screw that," she said flatly, trying to step around him.

The night air lifted her scent. It surrounded him, mixing with the sweet evening aromas of fresh grass and recent rain. Though distracted, he reached out, stopping her again. He knew he shouldn't.

"So now what? What next?" he asked.

They were close. She looked up at him, and the irritation in her face melted into something else. Bo didn't know if it was his imagination or wishful thinking, but heat arced between them the way it had back in the bar.

The way it always had.

"I don't understand this," she said, stuttering a bit, unsure. Rattled.

"What don't you understand?"

"Why I— What this *thing* is with you."

"What thing would that be, exactly?"

"Why I feel…when we… I don't know you. I don't even think I like you much," she said, shaking her head. "But when I look at you, I…"

She remembered. Or some part of her did.

He took her chin between his forefinger and thumb.

Bo's heartbeat was racing, too. He should walk away, call a cab and leave. He should let this be.

But he wasn't going to.

"I think I know what you mean. I feel it, too," he said, his voice a whisper.

Her eyes widened, and without warning she turned her cheek into his palm. The light rub of her skin on his set his blood on fire, and sense evaporated. Everything was lost to the night except being close to her, finally. Bo wanted to be closer.

He put his hand at the back of her neck, bringing her forward until she bumped up against him. Then they were kissing, and it was the first time he could breathe in months.

He thought it would be a quick, gentle kiss, but need came on so hot and sudden it knocked all the sense out of him. Her arms wrapped around him, and she was pressing into him as she always had, as hungry as he was.

Bo pulled her in tighter, parting her lips and kissing her as passionately as he could. Still it wasn't enough.

She was breathing hard as he slipped his hand along the small of her back, up under the edge of her shirt. Her skin was cool from the night air.

He explored her throat before working his way up to her lips again, but she pulled away, as if suddenly realizing what was happening. At the same time, voices rose in the lot behind them.

Bo couldn't think straight. He reached for her again. "Erin, don't—"

She pushed past him and ran down the sidewalk.

He stared after her, cursed under his breath, some little thread of clarity returning.

What had he just done?

If his place in the investigation had been iffy before, he'd just made it a lot worse. No one knew about his previous relationship with Erin—they'd seen each other in off-hours, never telling anyone. If the department found out now, well, things could get complicated. At best, they'd take him off the case. At worst…well, he didn't want to think about it.

They could think he was covering for her. They could think he was ethically compromised in any number of ways.

As he strode through the lot, reaching for his phone with slightly shaking hands, he couldn't help one thought that kept going around in the back of his head as her scent and taste still lingered. No matter what happened, it had been worth it.

2

ERIN DREW HER hand back quickly as she saw the blood well on her fingertip.

"Stupid thorns."

She was sorting roses for arrangements, making sure only the perfect, healthiest ones made it into the bouquets. Her fingers were freezing, but she couldn't do the work with gloves, so she'd risked the thorns.

Rinsing off the wound, she grabbed a paper towel from the rack and held it until it stopped bleeding. It was only one of about a dozen scrapes and punctures she'd gotten from the flowers that day.

Working for a florist wasn't something she wanted to do, but it was *something* to do. She wasn't a paid employee, but Kit said she could always use the free help, and at least it kept her busy. Erin couldn't hole up in her house all day doing nothing until her memory came back. Then she really would go crazy.

However, even the prickly thorns didn't take her mind off Bo Myers.

Maybe she was fumbling the flowers so much because she hadn't slept all night, and when she did doze off, he was kissing her again. And more.

Much, much more.

She'd dreamed of him before in hazy, undefined ways, but last night... Well, her imagination had had a lot more material to work with. Her fantasies had been very specific. She remembered the whorls of dark hair on his chest as her fingers had touched him. The hard muscles of his thigh and in particular, a mark on the side of his hip that her mind returned to again and again. It was shaped like an almond, dark against his normal skin tone.

She'd pressed her lips to it, hearing him moan as her hands explored elsewhere.

And there had been apples.

Usually, her dreams were smoky and shapeless, everything occurring in jumbles against a blurred background. But last night she'd seen apples. As if she were looking up from the ground, under a tree full of ripe, red fruit.

When he'd kissed her outside the bar, it had been a surprise, but on a deeper, more basic level, it had been familiar and *right*.

Her hands trembled as she returned to the roses, sorting them by variety without further injury and putting them in fresh water and into the coolers. Then she headed out front, where she saw that the closed sign had been flipped and her sister was bent over the computer on the counter.

"Evening already? What time is it?"

"Four-thirty. I closed a bit early."

Kit—short for Kathleen, a name that Erin learned her sister had never liked—looked up from her work, eyeing the front of Erin's shirt with a smirk. "The roses biting again?"

"How could you... Oh," she said, looking down to see blood from various scrapes had gotten on the white blouse she wore.

"I told you to wear one of the aprons," Kit said in true older-sister, know-it-all tone. So what if she had been right?

"I will next time, *Kathleen*," Erin said with appropriate sisterly sarcasm.

Kit's lips twitched with humor.

"Well, it's good that you remember how to be annoying."

Erin stuck her tongue out and they laughed. Joking around was good and helped dispel some of the ghosts she'd been wrestling with—and her thoughts about Bo.

"Do you mind if I take off early, too?"

Kit looked at Erin over the top of her glasses, frowning. "You're going out with the guys from the firehouse again?"

Tension settled between them, as Erin struggled between telling Kit what happened and telling her she wasn't her mother. Erin could go where she wanted, including out with the crew.

Kit had told her outright that she'd never been a fan of Erin's chosen profession. The accident had made her even more set against it. Kit didn't even seem to like her hanging out with the guys, but Erin enjoyed seeing them. She wondered what her sister would think about what happened with Bo.

"I can tell something is bothering you. Spill." Kit was way too perceptive.

Erin chose her words carefully. "Do you know if I

was seeing anyone before the accident? If there was a guy? Someone special?"

Kit's eyebrows rose. "I don't think so. You were all about the job and never mentioned anyone. Did you remember something?"

"I don't know. Maybe. I've been having some dreams, and I can't tell if it's a memory or a figment of my imagination, but I saw someone at the bar last night, and he was...familiar."

"How so?"

"You know. Familiar," Erin said again, with an emphasis that made her sister nod knowingly.

"Well, I suppose you might have hooked up with someone and not said anything. But you never told me about it, not that you would have."

Erin frowned. Apparently, she and Kit had not exactly been close sisters, though Kit had been there for her every minute since the accident. Whatever tension was between them didn't matter when the chips were down.

"Did he know you?"

Erin nodded. "There was definite chemistry. The explosive kind."

Erin couldn't remember anything about sex, not since making out with her senior year boyfriend in high school and letting him get her bra off. That was her last clear memory.

It was disconcerting, not knowing her sexual history. She'd been on birth control at the time of the fire, so she must have had an active sex life, but she couldn't remember any of it.

"Well, what did he say?"

"Um, not much, really. I kind of bolted before we talked."

Kit's expression was sympathetic. "I know this is hard for you, and it has to be frightening to bump into people, especially men, who might know you better than you know yourself, but maybe he could help. Maybe if you talked with him, he could help you remember. Was he a member of the department?"

"Yeah, he was. We talked, and I left. I guess I, well... Last night was weird."

"Talk to him if you get a chance. But make sure there are other people around, you know, the usual safety drill."

Erin had been thinking the same thing. It was clear that there was something between her and the fire marshal, but the only one who could tell her what was Bo. But if they had been an item, why had he kept it secret until now?

"Or maybe it's better if you don't," Kit said, changing gears. "Being with the guys so often at the firehouse could be a bad idea. You should be moving forward, not get stuck in the past."

Erin couldn't help the irritation that her sister's comment spawned. "They're my only friends. And they help. If I can get my memory back—"

"I think you have to face that you're not going back to that job."

"There's a chance, if I can get my memory back—"

Kit shook her head. "I'm sorry, honey, I know you loved it, but it would be like starting from scratch, even if you do remember."

"Then that's what I'll do."

"Being with them gives you false hope. Keeps you

from finding something new. I don't know why you'd want to go back to being a firefighter anyway. It nearly killed you."

Kit's features tightened with fear and grief, and Erin's heart softened. The nurses said that her sister had been by Erin's bedside every day at the hospital. Some nights, too, when things were iffy about her condition. Kit had also taken care of their mother when she was dying, and ran her own business while she was helping Erin.

Erin tried to imagine what it was like for people having to deal with her accident and her amnesia, but she was also tired of feeling responsible for it. She really didn't agree with her sister about hanging out with the guys—it didn't give her false hope. It gave her some sense of stability. But she could understand her sister's fear.

"I'm sorry it was so hard for you. And I'm grateful you've let me be here with you. It's nice to spend time together. I assume we didn't do that so much before?"

Kit sighed, the strain melting away somewhat. "No, we didn't. Sometimes we'd have lunch on your days off, but even then, you were usually at the firehouse. I'd meet you there."

"I'm sorry. The more I hear, the more I know that I gave everything to the job. Maybe too much. But I *do* appreciate it. And I appreciate you. I really do."

Erin closed the distance to hug her sister.

Kit hugged her back. "I'm not trying to be critical. I know they're your friends. But I worry about your future."

"It's only been a few months since I've been out of the hospital. I'm not giving up yet on getting my past back. I don't know what I'll do with my life, and the job, but right now I need to remember. I have to have hope, false or otherwise."

"Okay. But maybe you can find a safer line of work next time?"

Erin held up her scraped fingers. "Like handling flowers? I'm willing to bet I didn't end up this bloody on a daily basis as a firefighter."

Kit couldn't resist a grin, shaking her head. "True, you are not a natural florist."

"What are you doing tonight?" Erin asked, changing the topic.

"Quarterly taxes for the store are almost due. I'm way behind on accounting."

Erin felt a pinch of guilt; her sister was behind, no doubt because of her.

"Another night working? So I take it you're not seeing anyone right now, either?"

Kit rolled her eyes. "The market has been down lately."

Erin chuckled. "Tomorrow night, I'm taking you to dinner."

"That sounds nice."

"Great. It's a date."

Erin left, glad the tension had lifted. With her sister anyway. She was one big knot inside at the thought of seeing Bo again.

Her watch told her that she might already be too late to catch him at his office. There was no way she could get home to change and then head over to the station, but she didn't want to wait until tomorrow.

When she reached her car, the decision was made for her as her cell phone rang. She looked down to see Bo's caller ID. Not his name, just "Fire Investigation," which was how he'd been labeled in her work contact list. If they did have a personal relationship, there was very little evidence of it. Wouldn't there have been emails or phone calls? A cute picture of him on her phone?

"Hello?"

"Erin."

"Marshal Myers."

"Bo, please."

She hadn't used his first name before, but considering she might have ended up having sex with him on the picnic table outside the bar if no one had interrupted the night before, she supposed they were way past formalities.

"I was hoping you might be able to meet me. To talk, if you have time," he said, breaking into her thoughts.

Hearing his voice made her think of his lips. His lips made her think of—

She ruthlessly cut off that line of thought. "I was thinking the same thing, actually. I'm leaving the shop now. I could be at your office in—"

"No, not the office. Your place?"

She paused. Was this smart? Why didn't he want to meet at his office, which was a safe, neutral ground? Did she feel comfortable enough with Bo to invite him to her house?

In a sense, no. She wasn't sure that what they had to talk about was fodder for public ears, either.

"How about that diner by the lake? June's?" she suggested. It had booths in the back, enough privacy to talk, but it was public enough so that they wouldn't, well, whatever.

He was so quiet she thought that he might have hung up.

"Are you there?"

"That works. An hour?"

"Okay, yes. That's good."

They hung up without further discussion.

The hour would give her time to go home, wash up and change her shirt, but as she stood in front of her closet twenty minutes later, she froze, unable to choose what to wear. All of the clothes she'd picked out with Dana now seemed too sexy—too inviting.

But she didn't want to wear any of her department shirts—that felt like a lie.

She growled in frustration, disgusted. She was meeting him at a diner, and it wasn't a date. They were going to talk. That was all. She didn't need to dress to impress.

Taking a blue blouse from the hanger, she put it on with the jeans she was already wearing and didn't bother checking in the mirror lest she change her mind. It would be fine. She lifted her hand to her hair, a reflex making her try to push it behind her ear. She kept forgetting it was short.

Locking the house, she took off and arrived at the diner just in time. The fire department SUV that Bo drove was already parked in the lot. He was early.

Her heartbeat picked up pace, and her hands were actually sweating. Damn.

"Oh, get over yourself, Riley," she muttered under her breath.

Getting out of the car, she slammed the door harder than she meant to. Nerves. She calmed herself, then walked inside.

Bo was at the back—apparently having had the same thought she did about privacy—though June's wasn't too full tonight. All the booths around them were empty, and she stepped forward. He was talking to a server who was putting a drink and menus on the table, and he smiled at the young waitress.

There was no flirtation—it was simply a friendly smile—but it tripped Erin up. He was in his uniform this time and that alone was striking. But that smile. It was killer. And it was for someone else.

A sharp pinch—jealousy?—grabbed at her chest. On the way to the booth, she passed the server who winked at her as she blew her bangs up, as if needing to cool down.

"Nice to see you again, hon. It's been a while."

The waitress had already hurried past by the time Erin could reply. She approached Bo with what she hoped was a casual, friendly smile.

"Hi. I hope you haven't been waiting long. I needed to go home and change. Crazy as it seems, I manage to make more of a mess of myself working with flowers than I probably did when I fought fires."

Oh, cripes, she was babbling.

He looked so good, sitting there in his uniform shirt, those long fingers wrapped around a coffee mug.

"It's only been few minutes. Thanks for agreeing to meet me."

So few words, and yet he managed to make her knees shake. She sat and found that she suddenly had nothing to say. Maybe this wasn't a good idea after all.

How the heck did she tell this man that she'd been having hot and heavy dreams about him, and she

needed to know if they'd ever had sex? Jumping right
in was the only option that came to mind.

"THE WAITRESS KNEW me. She seemed to know...us. Was
there an...us?"

"We used to come here now and then," Bo hedged,
taken aback by her sudden question. She was clearly
nervous, and he was now doubting the wisdom of meeting again. Especially here.

He was unsure how much to share. Last night he'd
shared way too much.

"With other people, like at the bar? Or together?"

Jill, the server, returned with Erin's drink, which
he'd ordered on reflex. His error became apparent when
she stared at the Coke and lime twist for a second, then
met his eyes knowingly.

"How long were we together?"

He blew out a breath and leaned into the table, clasping his hands tighter around the mug as he rested forward on his elbows.

"Almost a year. Maybe I should have told you, but...
it didn't seem like it would help. You'd been through
enough, and I had a job to do. It didn't seem...relevant."

Her eyebrows flew up, and he saw the pulse flut-
tering hard in her throat. She reached for her soda and
took several long draws.

"Are you okay?"

She put the glass down with a sigh. "I'm fine. After
last night, maybe even before, I knew, on some level,
but I never thought...a year? I thought it might have
been a hookup or something. There's nothing that
would have made me think we were dating, not for

that long. No pictures, nothing in my home of yours… nothing."

"You weren't sentimental that way, and it was over well before your accident. You probably took me off your email and phone. But you were also paranoid about anyone finding out, so we didn't really text or stuff like that. Anyway, last night is what I wanted to talk to you about. I was out of line. I'd had too much to drink. No excuse, of course. But I wanted to know if you were going to file a report."

She frowned. "What kind of report? I've already given my statement, and I don't know what else—"

"A report on me, Erin. A complaint. About what happened."

"Why? Why would I do that?"

She sounded completely shocked, and he withheld his response as their food arrived. He wasn't really that hungry. He hadn't slept at all the night before, no wonder, and he'd been a growling bear all day. His supervisor wanted Erin's case closed, unsolved. There were others he needed to get to, but he couldn't let this go. Someone had hurt her; Bo was going to find out who it was, if he had to do it on his own free time.

Whatever it took.

"I shouldn't have done what I did. I know I'm all but a stranger to you, no matter what happened in our past. I had no right. I wanted to apologize, but I understand if you want to report it. I wanted to let you know that."

Unlike him, Erin dug into her spaghetti dinner as though it was going to save her from certain death. She'd always been a stress eater. He didn't know where she put it, she was so slim, but she always could eat as much as any of the guys on the crew.

He thought this would be easier. A professional meeting in a public place. He wanted to apologize and reassure her it wouldn't happen again. Still, she had a right to file a formal report. She was a member of the department, and he was investigating an incident in which she was involved. It was his job to let her know she had recourse.

"I don't want to file a report, and you have nothing to apologize for. I wasn't exactly fighting you off."

She said it with a wry grimace, as if more disappointed with herself than him.

"Erin, if I scared you, or hurt you—"

"You did neither." Her eyes met his squarely, but then she looked down, unsure again. "I think though… I need to ask you something."

"Shoot."

"Do you have a mark or a scar on your hip? Almond-shaped?"

Bo's heart skipped a beat. "Yeah, I do. A birthmark. You were always fascinated with it for some reason."

She fumbled her fork and nearly dropped it to the table as she caught her breath, audibly.

"Erin?"

She closed her eyes briefly, as if working up the courage to speak. Her newly short hair sharpened the angles of her cheekbones and her jaw, making her green eyes and her lips look larger and lusher than before. He'd always loved her long brown hair, wrapping it around his fingers and watching it fall over her shoulders, but he liked this new look, too. How it exposed the long lines of her throat and the curve of her neck and collarbone. The soft flesh of her earlobes.

He grabbed for his coffee, his mouth gone dry.

"Tell me what's wrong."

She lifted her gaze to his, and this time, it wasn't veiled or distant, but...there was a spark. She almost smiled.

"I *remembered* that, then. I remembered...after last night. I remembered a lot. It wasn't just dreams."

He straightened, his attention sharpened. "About the fire?"

She shook her head. "No. Not that. Things about you. Like the birthmark. I wasn't sure if I was just fantasizing, but...apparently it was real. I can't believe that I really remembered something!"

Paired with the astonished joy in her expression was the rosy flush of embarrassment. Because she was saying that she had remembered them together—having sex. Naked, since she remembered the birthmark.

"You dreamed about me?"

He didn't mean to ask aloud, but she'd taken him a bit by surprise, too.

Erin nodded. "Before last night, even. And I keep seeing...apples. Like there were apple trees somewhere."

"We made love in a local orchard once."

"Wow. That's...daring."

He smiled, warmth stirring at the memory. "We were alone. Except for some cows in the next field, but they didn't care."

"Where was our first date?"

He couldn't look away from her. "Here."

"Oh."

The significance of her choosing this place tonight seemed to dawn on her.

"So we broke up?"

"We did."

"Amicably?"

"Mostly, I guess."

He said the words tersely, unsure what else to say. He wasn't about to lay himself open for her again, not like this. Not to satisfy her curiosity.

"Why?"

"Why what?"

"Why did we break up? Did we have a fight? Did one of us cheat? Step out?"

He shook his head at the unthinkable, but somewhere in his mind, he wondered. They did have some arguments, because he knew—he sensed—that she was keeping something from him over the month or so before their breakup. He never found out what, but he knew she hadn't been seeing someone else. He was sure of it.

"No, no cheating."

"Then what?"

Everything inside Bo tensed. He really didn't want to peel the scab off this wound, but he could respect her need to know.

"I wanted more, you didn't."

"More of what?"

"More of you, more than we had. More than you were willing to give."

"What does that mean?"

"We were seeing each other in secret. We called it being discreet, since we worked together, but when I wanted people to know, you didn't."

"Why?"

"You were worried the guys would start to treat

you differently. Act differently. That it would affect your work."

She was quiet for a few seconds, her lips turning downward.

"So this was my fault?"

"It wasn't anyone's fault. It just ran its course."

"Wow, okay. Well. So we're…friends?"

"No. Last night should have shown you that we could never be friends. We…avoided each other. It was easier when I moved up to arson."

She nodded, looking uncomfortable again.

"I should go. I wanted to apologize and let you know I know I was wrong, and that you had the right to report what happened. It won't happen again, if that helps." His tone was formal, stiffened by painful memories and desire he couldn't do one damned thing about.

He took out his wallet and paid their check.

"If you do remember anything else, about the fire, that is, please call the office. You can always talk to my assistant if I'm not in."

He slid out of the booth, heading toward the door. Heard her feet on the tile floor behind him.

She caught up with him outside, before he reached his truck.

"Bo, wait. Please."

It was still light out as she followed him down the side of his SUV, between the cars.

He turned on her. "I can't do this, Erin."

He might as well be honest about it.

"Do what?"

"Talk about old times. Tell you all about us. It's over, and I can't see the point in raking back over it."

"I hurt you."

She stated it like a fact, emotionless, studying his face. Bo didn't want her to see, but he supposed that horse was already out of the barn.

"It's fine. Over and done."

She put a hand on his arm. "I'm sorry. For that, and for making you go back over this. From my dreams… from what I can remember, what we had was deep. I can feel it, even if I can't remember it all."

Erin stepped in closer. She didn't look nervous anymore. She was…something else. Bo froze, keys in hand.

"I don't want to play games. Or be played with," he said, his voice almost desperate as he swallowed hard, his breath short.

"I don't want to play games, either. I want to remember," she said softly, and leaned into him, hips first. Her hands drifted up his torso, over his chest to his shoulders as she pressed in closer.

A second later she was kissing him, and everything else fell away. She dropped gentle, easy kisses along his jaw, as if getting to know it again, mapping him with her lips. He swallowed, turning his face away, trying to get control. To resist. So she burrowed into the hollow of his throat, her tongue darting out to taste him.

He groaned her name. She sighed against him.

"If we parted ways, why does this all feel so right?" she asked, nibbling her way back up to his mouth.

Bo dropped his keys as his arms came around her, and his resolve crumbled, reversing their positions and pressing her into the side of the SUV, his mouth hungry for hers.

He slid one hand up under her blouse, his palm settling over her breast. She arched into the touch, an invitation. If this kept happening, they were going to end up naked in the back of his truck as they had the first time they'd left this diner and couldn't keep their hands off each other.

"History repeating itself," he muttered before he sank into another kiss. So much for good intentions.

3

"WE HAVE TO STOP," Bo said against her mouth, his hands on her shoulders, pushing her away.

Erin's entire being protested, and she shook her head.

"No."

Then his big hands were on her face, making her look at him. His cheeks were ruddy, his eyes hot. There was no doubt that he wanted her.

"I'm not going to do this. It's taking advantage, don't you get that? You're not in any state of mind to be making these decisions."

That riled her. She might have lost her memory, but she wasn't so incapacitated that she couldn't decide if she wanted a man or not. Granted, there were a few extra things going on that might influence whether she wanted *this* man, but still.

She dropped a hand, planted it between them as she closed her fingers around the erection that bulged against his slacks.

"Erin, don't," he almost begged, even as he pressed into her.

She took her hand away, shaken by the desperate look on his face. She'd hurt this man, and even if she couldn't remember it, she was doing it again.

Shame welled, and she stopped touching him, dropping her forehead against his chest.

"I'm sorry. I—I really want you, though. It's…crazy, but I do."

"I know. I want you, too."

"I could tell."

He bit out a short laugh, his hands still on her shoulders, squeezing lightly.

Her eyes closed, inhaling his scent, feeling the heat of his body, Erin tried to calm her own need, but her mind had different ideas.

"Oh," she whispered in surprise.

"What?"

"I can almost smell them, the apples. What the heck is it about the apples, Bo?"

Then she knew. As if she'd known it all the time. She pulled back to look up at him. "It was the last time we were together, wasn't it? The last time we made love?"

His jaw tightened, and he nodded before his head dropped back, staring upward at the sky as he answered. "Yeah."

The simple confirmation made another puzzle piece click into place. "So this is June…I was out of commission mid-February through April, and we broke up a month before the explosion, you said. January? So how could we have been in an orchard?"

"It was in October. Our last time. Then I left to train for the new job and came back at Christmas. We officially broke up shortly after that."

Something pulled at the far side of her memory, but she couldn't reach it and groaned in frustration.

"I can feel it's all there, like it's behind a wall, but I can't get to it," she said, closing her fists into his shirt, an expression of frustration more than desire this time.

His arms came around her, holding her close.

But it had happened again. Being close to him loosened up her mind, her reservations, or whatever. Memories, no matter how sketchy, started to form. Whatever he'd been to her, it was strong enough to pull her back in a way nothing else had been.

"It'll be okay, Duck," he said, and she thought he kissed her hair.

Her head came up quickly.

"Duck. You always called me that. Why?"

Blood raced through her veins, excitement coursing through her as she remembered another small thing.

"You were always hitting your head on the bar above the seat in the hook and ladder, and I had to remind you to duck so many times, I started calling you that."

His thumb was rubbing over her jaw, a tender gesture in the wake of the passion that had carried them away a few seconds earlier, though that was still there, too.

She measured her words carefully.

"You said you wanted more from me. I want more, too…from you. Now."

Her eyes met his, and she hoped he knew what she was asking.

Desire flared in the brown depths of his gaze. Of course he knew.

"It's not a good idea."

"Why not? Whatever it is between us, it's the only

thing that's made me remember *anything*. And if I can remember you, and us, maybe I can remember other things."

He smiled slightly, a hint of bitterness there as he dropped his hands from her shoulders and moved away, bending to grab his keys from the ground.

"Erin, as much as I'd like to help, I'm not about to sleep with you to see if it can help jog your memory. Thanks anyway."

She took a step back, giving him some space.

"It's not like that, not exactly," she tried to explain, though she supposed it was exactly like that. She did want to use him, in many delightful ways, and if it got her memory back, even better.

"What is it like, then?"

He caught her gaze, and she grimaced in the face of his challenge.

"Okay, yes, it is about getting my memory back. Can you blame me? I want my life back. My work. My sense of damned purpose," she said in frustration. "But I think there's more to it than that. For both of us. These dreams…they've been with me since the hospital. I didn't know what they were, but they get stronger, more…insistent. And I can see in your face that…you want me."

He pulled up straight, his body tensing. "That doesn't mean I should have you."

"No, but I think all of this might mean that we left things…wrong. Unsettled. There are still issues between us that need to be…addressed."

His eyes narrowed, pinning her. "And you think we should *address* these issues in bed?"

Her cheeks burned, but she didn't let him put her off.

She took a step forward, laid her hand on his chest. "In bed, or wherever else seems right. From what you tell me, and from what I dream about, we weren't exactly... conventional in our choice of places to have sex. Were there others? Other public places? What did I like, Bo? What did I want you to do to me? I don't remember... but I want to find out."

Erin knew she was pushing him, this man she hardly knew, but she also knew it was right. Deep inside, this felt like the right thing to do. She had to get him to see that, to get him past his doubts and uncooperative stance.

"You can't remember anything. How can you know what you want?"

"I know I want you. It's one of the few things I do know. It's not taking advantage, Bo. I'm fully aware of what I'm doing, and what I'm asking for."

"Do you? Really, Erin? Do you know what you're asking from me? After you walked away from us? After you were almost killed? You've looked at me— or rather, looked past me—for months, like a stranger. Do you really know what you're asking?"

His expression was fierce, and Erin was nearly knocked out of her certainty by the frankness of his objections. What he said was true. This wasn't just about her, but she needed to push anyway. She was desperate. He was her only hope to remember anything. To recapture what she once had.

"Maybe it would be different this time. I'm not sure. I only know that I need you, and I think you need me. You said you wanted more from me. I'll give you anything you want, Bo...whatever you need. If you give me...this. Give me a chance to get my life back."

He shook his head at her and got into his truck without another word. Erin's heart, and her hopes, sank. Her eyes burned as he started the engine.

She'd lost. She'd lost Bo and a whole lot more than that.

He sat in the driver's seat with the engine running, not moving.

She didn't move, either. Holding her breath that he'd get back out. Change his mind.

He looked out the window at her.

"I'm sorry, Erin, but I don't think this will work. You'll need to find another way. From now on, please contact my assistant if you need anything."

It was all he said, backing up and driving out of the lot.

Erin didn't realize she was crying until a breeze picked up and made her aware of the cool sting of tears on her cheeks. She got back to her car, sat there until it got dark. She'd taken her last shot and lost. Maybe her memory would come back, and maybe it wouldn't, but Bo clearly wasn't going to be part of it.

Maybe Kit was right. Maybe she had to stop clinging to this foolish hope and the past. It really was time to move on.

Bo STARED BLINDLY at the email that filled his computer screen as he sat at his desk the next morning. It was early, and no one was in yet. He hadn't slept again. Not after hours of self-recriminations about backing away from Erin. It had been the right thing to do, but it wasn't what he wanted.

This, the content of the email, was supposed to be what he wanted. An offer he'd been working for his entire life—a job with the FBI's Critical Incident Response Group. He'd helped them a few times as a cop and once recently as an investigator.

He'd use everything he'd ever learned and take it all to the next level. They were asking him back for a final interview, and if it went well, they wanted him to start in August. In Virginia.

He rubbed his hand over his tired eyes, wondering why he didn't feel happier. This was important to him. Since his uncle had been seriously injured in the Pentagon on 9/11, it was all Bo had lived for. Until Erin.

She had made him believe that he lived for something else. For someone else. For a while anyway.

Erin's face, her desperation, her crushing disappointment as he'd left the night before, played in his mind's eye again.

"Damn it." He closed the email, got up and went to get himself another cup of coffee, and went to check out the morning's reports, but he couldn't concentrate.

Could helping Erin remember their past relationship trigger her ability to remember other things, perhaps the fire, or anything she saw that could help them? She'd seemed so sure that being with him would help her remember. Or maybe Bo was finding convenient connections, rationalizations to be with her, when he knew it wasn't ethical.

He felt like a jerk no matter what he decided. If he did as she asked, he was taking advantage of her situation to have sex with her, no matter how much she said that wasn't the case. She was desperate to get her memory back, but just because she'd remembered a few tidbits about him—them—it didn't mean that being with him would fuel any more recollections.

But walking away had been hard. She needed him, and she was right—he needed her, too. He'd tried to pull that need out by the root, but he'd failed. Their last few interactions had proved that.

They'd left things unsaid, and they'd never had any real closure. Maybe that's why she'd been so difficult to get over, even after all this time. And he wanted her so damned badly. It would be too easy to take what she was offering, and what then?

For her, it was only sex. She wanted him—he knew that, he could feel it. But she was just scratching an itch while trying to get her past back—and if that happened, she'd just remember that she hadn't wanted him before. Maybe she'd hate him even more for doing this.

Or maybe something would be different? She'd hinted at that. And she did seem…different. Some things were still the same, but there was no doubt that she'd been through a life-altering experience.

Could it have altered what she wanted from life? What she wanted from him?

The chances of her ever going back to firefighting were slim. She had to know that. Even if her memory came back, her physical status after the brain surgeries and her psychological state would all need to be re-evaluated. Would the crew trust her as they did before? Could she even walk into a fire, or would she freeze?

He put the reports aside and looked at his computer again. He'd done some research on the brain damage that she'd suffered, and more reading on amnesia. It was a highly specialized topic. There were different forms of forgetting and different reasons people lost their memories.

Erin had what was typically called retrograde amnesia—she'd forgotten everything but her childhood memories up until college. But as Bo read through one particularly interesting medical report online, a theory formed in his mind. He found the number of a psychologist he knew who served the police and the fire departments, and called the number, finding himself on the line with Dr. Newcomb minutes later.

"How can I help you, Marshal?"

"I'm investigating the arson case that killed a fireman in February, and left one with serious brain damage and memory loss. I was wondering if you had a second to answer some questions."

"I do. I remember the case. I talked with Erin Riley. That's in the report, so it's not protected information, though I can't share any of what we spoke about, of course."

"Of course. I wanted to ask you about the type of amnesia Erin has. Her neurologist called it retrograde amnesia, caused by the head trauma she suffered, and probably from the brain surgeries, as well."

"Yes, I recall. I've never had a patient with nearly complete amnesia. Is she doing well?"

"I thought you said you were talking to her?"

"Only three times after she left the hospital, and then she opted not to come back."

Bo smirked. Sounded like Erin. She never did like doctors.

"I was reading up on it on the internet, and I wondered if the neurologist could have had it wrong. I was reading about a kind of amnesia called dissociative amnesia, where she could be blocking something traumatic—something stressful that her brain doesn't want to remember. Could it be that instead? Do you think she could have seen something at the fire that was so traumatizing that she doesn't want to remember it?"

"It's possible, though usually dissociative amnesia wouldn't be so encompassing. She might block the event, or things related to it, but not her entire life for over a decade."

"I see. Is it possible to have both? Perhaps the brain damage made what would otherwise just be selective forgetting much worse?"

"Hmm. It's definitely possible. Why do you think this could be the case?"

"I'm not a doctor, of course, but Erin has been remembering a few details regarding a long-term relationship she had—and she thinks that if she could be with the person in that relationship, she might remember more. Is that possible?"

"It's a very good sign that she's remembered anything—that's promising. It could take days or years, there's no telling. The brain is unpredictable. But triggers are a key factor—if there's a strong enough trigger, something so important to her, or so deep in her mind that she's recollecting it, it's certainly wise to pursue that. There's no way to know what or how much she might recall, but it's certainly possible that opening one strong channel of memory could lead to more recollections. And if she is repressing memories that are too frightening to recall, being with someone who makes her feel safe could help that rise to the surface, as well."

"Thank you, Doctor. I'll let her know."

"Marshal Myers, please tell Erin she's welcome in my office anytime, especially if she's going through anything unsettling in this process. I'd love to work with her if she needs more support."

"I'll tell her. Thank you."

Bo hung up, not sure if he should have made an appointment with the doctor. He probably needed his head examined for considering this, but it sounded as though it actually could be possible. That being with Erin could actually bring her memories back.

If that was the case, how could he move on with his life, into his future, and leave her behind without at least trying to help her get her life back, too?

Glancing up as other members of the office arrived, chatter floated in the door, and he smelled fresh coffee brewing. He got up and closed his door, needing to think.

He could potentially help Erin remember—maybe remember everything.

Was he really considering this?

He knew going in this time that there wouldn't be any real reconciliation. They were still "over"— nothing would change that.

He had other plans, too—the job in Virginia, for starters. He'd be here for only a bit more than two months if he got the job. Less than that, since he'd have to give notice and get someone new to take his place here. His assistant was good, but he wasn't ready to move up the ranks yet.

So that meant Bo had a month or so, just a few weeks, to cram in as much of their relationship as he could in hopes it might make her remember everything.

He just had to keep straight on the fact that he wasn't in it this time for the long haul, either. It could be just sex for him, too. A way to get her out of his system?

Closure. A way to leave things better between them than they had before.

It was also a chance to close the case, potentially. Maybe a way to save lives, since they still had an arsonist out there who hadn't been caught. What if Erin had seen something or experienced something that could help them find the person who had set that fire?

He knew he was talking himself into it, but it also made sense. There were more good reasons to take this risk than not to.

He'd already dialed her number, his phone in hand. He was surprised when she picked up.

"I thought you might not answer." He didn't bother with hellos.

"I didn't see who it was first."

She sounded tired. And cranky. For some reason, that made him smile. She was always irritable when she woke up.

"I'm sorry I was hard on you last night. Listen, I want to help if I can. Are you free today?"

"Say when."

Her tone perked up considerably. Bo closed his eyes, steadying his breathing. This felt surreal.

"I'm taking the rest of the day off. I've got a few things to sort out. How about if I come by your place later?"

"Okay. I'll be here."

She sounded nervous now, too. "I just want to talk, Erin. We need to talk about it…first."

"Okay. Sure. Good."

With that, they hung up. Bo packed his stuff and told his assistant to beep him only if there was an emergency. Then he was in his truck, thinking about

Erin, wondering if he wasn't making a huge mistake. It wasn't the first time he'd done that, and probably wouldn't be the last.

KIT STOOD BY the door as she scanned the crowd for Erin's cap of shiny brown hair. It was hard to see anyone in the busy crowd.

This was the place Erin usually went with her firehouse buddies, so it was where Kit figured she'd find her, but as far as she could see, there was no Erin.

She was doubly disappointed, having needed the break from her own worries. The past few months had been a balancing act, largely tilted to the side of addressing Erin's crisis, which was obviously huge. But Kit had her own troubles to deal with. Her flower shop wasn't doing well these days, especially with more people ordering flowers online or getting them at the local grocery stores. She'd been holding it together for a while, but she'd lost one large account last month, and the individual, walk-in business was dropping off, as well. In addition, getting good quality, fair-trade flowers wasn't inexpensive.

Most consumers had no idea that the flowers they bought at many outlets or online at discount prices were often shipped from countries that farmed the blooms and exploited local people, usually women, to keep prices down and their own profits up. Kit supported only fair-trade suppliers, and that meant her flowers were more expensive than most, but she included fair-trade information with all purchases. She found that her customers liked knowing they were buying flowers that truly helped people instead of subjugating them.

But in the troubled economy, being socially conscious was often a luxury.

All Kit had ever wanted to do was run a flower shop. It was her dream, since she was a little girl. She'd worked at one as a teenager, and she used the college money left to her by her parents to open the shop. It had done very well for a while. But times changed, and the internet, recessions and so forth were taking their toll on her dreams.

The shop and her sister were the most important things in her life—they were all she had left. Erin was young when their father had died of a heart attack at the station. He was always at the station. Lived and died there, literally. Their mother was gone eight years later. Erin had been out working on a fire when their mom passed away.

Sometimes Kit felt terribly alone. Feelings weren't always fair, she knew. Sometimes, they were awful, confusing things. Like when the doctors said that Erin had amnesia and very likely wouldn't return to fire-fighting.

Kit had, on some level, been happy about that. It wasn't very supportive, she knew that, but she was so happy to have Erin around again. But Erin seemed drawn to her old crew, even now. It was like an obsession.

As Kit moved farther into the room, she didn't see her sister anywhere, and her heart sank. So much for sister time.

"Hey, you're Riley's sister...the flower lady."

Kit turned toward the voice and found a very, *very* large man standing near a tall table, where he put a beer down and faced her, holding out his hand.

"I'm Hank Aaron."

She raised her eyebrows.

"No joke, that's my name. Dad was a huge baseball fan. Mom couldn't talk him out of it. And you're... Kathy?"

"Kathleen, but everyone calls me Kit." She smiled, looking into his face. "Now I remember. We met at the hospital a few times. I'm sorry. I was not quite coherent back then."

She reached out, shook his hand, which swallowed her own. His skin was rough, but not in an unpleasant way. It scraped on hers and made her wonder how those large hands would feel on the rest of her.

"Understandable. That was hell, waiting to see what would happen, especially for you. Families have it hard in our business. Can I get you a beer?"

She paused, took her hand back. She was going to say no. It was obvious Erin wasn't here, but then Kit changed her mind as her stomach rumbled.

"That would be nice, thanks. I might order something to eat, too. I was hoping to meet Erin here, but I guess she had other things to do."

Hank frowned. "Do you think she's okay?"

"I do. She shut off her phone. She does that when she wants to be left alone. I know what she's going through is so hard...and I don't know how to help most of the time. I try to give her space to figure things out, but I'm never quite sure what to do. Or if she needs me for anything at all."

She failed to keep the slight edge of resentment out of her tone, and Hank noticed.

"I imagine this is difficult for both of you. Riley, um, Erin hasn't been quite the same since she woke up.

We notice it, too. She's...I don't know. Like she's looking for something, I guess. There, and then not there."

"At least I get to see her more these days. I think you guys knew her better than I did before. She certainly spent more time with you all, and I know being around you now is a comfort to her. But I worry she's too caught in the past to move forward. She doesn't like hearing that, as you can imagine."

Hank drew himself up, all six feet who-only-knew-how-many-inches of him, and looked down at her with calm understanding. How did this big bear of a man come off so Zenlike? As he started to speak, she expected him to make excuses and find some means to escape her dumping all her problems on him. She never did that, not as a habit, and wouldn't blame him for wanting to get clear of her.

"Have you had anyone to talk to since this happened?" he asked instead.

A beer came, magically appearing in her hand. Hank said something to the woman that she couldn't hear over the noise.

"I ordered some dinner and got something for you, too."

Kit was taken aback at his presumptuousness, but then she acquiesced as she knew he meant no offense. And he would know what was good to eat here anyway.

"Thank you."

"C'mon, the back is quieter. It can get nuts around here on the weekend."

He led her to a table near the back, pulled out a chair for her and then sat himself. He looked sort of ridiculous at the small tavern table, being lumberjack-sized.

"So you didn't answer my question."

"What question was that?"

Kit started to relax a bit. It had been a long time since she'd been out for an evening, even longer since it had been in a bar with any member of the opposite sex. She'd needed a break more than she thought.

"Have you had a chance to talk to anyone about what's gone on with Erin? The department has counselors for us, and they work with family, too, when it's needed."

She shook her head. "I'm fine. I was just ticked off that she stood me up."

"Yeah, she gets caught up in her head these days. Can't blame her, but it's not easy to live with, either. None of this is. Our schedules, lifestyles…it's hard on loved ones."

"Yours, too?"

"I'm not married, if that's your way of asking. Or involved."

Kit's felt her cheek warm. "I wasn't asking, really, that's none of my—"

"Then it was my way of letting you know."

Kit stopped, flustered. "Oh. Okay."

Luckily, the server arrived with their food. Kit was immediately in love—with the chicken.

"Dig in. Don't be shy." Hank smiled, triggering another warm curl low in her belly that wasn't caused by the spicy aroma of the food.

Kit didn't hesitate, starting in on the chicken and handmade fries without reserve, licking her fingers when she was done. Hank was working his way through his, too, and eyed the remnants left on her plate.

"You and your sister both know how to eat, that's

for sure." He said it appreciatively, and Kit couldn't help but grin.

"Yeah, my parents believed in healthy eaters. Good thing they also passed on their active metabolisms."

"You are in nice shape," he said with a twinkle in his blue eyes.

She couldn't explain her response except that it had been a very long time since she'd been with a man. She was thirty-three, and had always imagined she'd be married with kids by now, but life hadn't made time for romance. It did, however, make time for lust and the occasional fling.

Things were definitely stirring here at the table between her and Hank. She wasn't sure when she stopped thinking about having a long-term relationship—her work, her parents, her sister…it all had consumed the years. Still, she enjoyed a night of hot sex now and then, when it was with the right guy.

But Hank wasn't the right guy. He was a firefighter, for one—definitely not her type—and he had worked with her sister. It was best, when scratching an itch, to have things as anonymous as possible. There was a good chance her path and Hank's could cross again, and that meant it would be a mistake to fan this little ember.

They used the wet wipes at the table to clean their hands, and Kit figured it was time to leave. She didn't want to send false signals by staying too long. She'd catch up with Erin tomorrow. She couldn't imagine where her sister was, but Kit's mood had mellowed on a full stomach.

Some live music started in the main room, though,

drowning out her voice. Hank said something, too, but she couldn't hear him, either.

"What?" she said loudly, her hand to her ear.

He smiled as he stood and reached his hand out to her in the universal invitation to dance.

Kit was momentarily stunned. What she wanted and what she should do were in opposition to each other.

What she wanted won. Just for tonight, she wanted to forget that she had to be at the shop at five in the morning and that she had responsibilities. That she had worries and troubles.

That there was no one to go home to.

She wanted to dance with Hank and enjoy her evening.

So she took his hand and let him lead her out to the floor, where he pulled her up close and proceeded to show her how well a big man could move.

4

ERIN WAS A knot of nerves and anxiety as she got ready for Bo to come over. He'd said they'd talk—and she knew they had to do that, but she wanted to do more.

Maybe.

She wanted to do whatever she needed to do to get this going between them.

"You're such a romantic," she said to herself, smirking in the mirror as she changed her shirt again, unable to decide if she should go with a bra or not.

She'd been with the man for a year. But for her, it was like a first date. A first time.

What had changed his mind?

Was she crazy? Throwing herself at him because it might prompt a few memories? When she was with him, next to him, she felt certain.

Less so right now.

When she heard his truck in the driveway, her hands went cold. She was being ridiculous. So nervous.

She reassured herself that Bo wouldn't do anything she didn't want to do. She knew that. He would leave this up to her. Maybe that was what was so difficult. It would be easier, in many ways, if he would just make the decisions. Take over.

The potential of *that* idea created a flutter in her pulse that got her out of the bedroom and down the stairs to meet him at the door.

She whipped it open before he even had a chance to knock.

"Hi." She was breathless.

He looked so serious; it didn't help with her nerves. "Hi."

He must have changed out of his uniform, now in a pair of jeans and a faded black T-shirt. He was carrying a box. The way he braced it in his arms made his biceps pop a bit, and Erin found herself staring.

"Can I come in?"

She stood back quickly, feeling foolish. "Certainly. Yes, come in. Sorry. I guess I'm surprised, still. I didn't expect you to call."

He faced her as she closed the door, and suddenly she wished her house was different. More cozy and inviting. When she'd come home from the hospital, even she'd been surprised at how sparse it was. She owned fewer than a dozen pieces of furniture, and the whole house was still painted in the plain beige that it probably was when she bought it. There were only a few pictures and some department awards on the walls, and her kitchen was lightly equipped. As though she barely lived here.

Now, the functional gray sofa in the living room looked cold and boring. Not like something you'd want to curl up on with someone.

Redecorating—and maybe repainting—definitely needed to be done.

"I know. You surprised me, too, last night, when we...talked. I guess I needed some time to cool down and think about...everything."

"Sure. I get that. What's in the box?"

He seemed surprised, as if he'd almost forgotten he was holding it.

"Oh, you mentioned that you didn't have any mementoes of our relationship here. You kept that kind of thing at my place, I guess, so people from the department wouldn't see anything if they came by here."

She frowned. "Was I really that secretive about it?"

"Can I put this down somewhere?"

"Yes, over on the table, please."

"You were concerned about what people would think, and not without reason. Our department has never had any problems, and the guys all think highly of you, the brass, too, but it's not unreasonable to assume they might have seen you differently if they found out we were together. And given our breakup, it was probably for the best that they didn't know. You were just being smart."

"I guess." But it still didn't seem right to her. It wasn't as if they were doing anything *wrong,* after all. Hadn't she proven herself on the job well enough to not worry about that kind of thing? Apparently not. "But anyway, I guess it doesn't matter now."

"No, it doesn't. But I thought maybe...well, that we could talk about this...arrangement we discussed. And that maybe seeing these items could trigger something for you, too."

Erin had to fend off a stab of disappointment. What did she think was going to happen? That he was going to jump her bones and get down to it as soon as he came through the door? Did he bring the box as a way of hoping she might remember without having to have sex with her?

She had a feeling that she wasn't used to feeling insecure. Not normally. It didn't sit well.

"This is weird, isn't it? You're my ex, and for me, this is like a first date. Maybe it was a mistake?"

She folded her arms, rubbing her upper arms, unsure.

He closed the space between them, placing an arm around her shoulders.

"It is strange. Awkward, for sure, which is why we don't have to do anything but talk. You call the shots. You set the pace, you say stop or go, yes or no—and I'll listen. Period. Okay?"

Some of her uneasiness drifted away as she looked at him, and she knew this was going to be okay.

"Yes, thanks. Do you want some coffee? I have some scrambled eggs leftover from breakfast, too, if you want them."

"Sure, that sounds good. I'll help myself if you want to grab the box."

Erin agreed. He probably knew his way around her kitchen as well as she did, given their past. Carrying the box to the sofa, she waited for him to open the box. When he sat down beside her, the box was between their feet on the floor.

She opened it, unsure what to expect. On top were several pictures in cheap but nice frames. She took them out and saw her and Bo, in various settings, and a few of them each alone.

"Wow," she said, swallowing hard as she went through them.

It was like looking at someone else, somebody else's pictures. Her heart clogged her throat at one of them on a beach, pressed up close, face-to-face.

Bo looked at her as if she was his world. She looked at him as if she wanted to be.

"Who took this?"

"I did. Auto-timer. I set it, and then run back to get in the shot before the camera goes off. It was always one of my favorites. Up at Lake Ontario. There's a nature center there with a private beach, and we'd go there now and then. Lots of tall rocks and places to prop the camera."

He reported the details as though they were just… details. Finishing his eggs, he set his plate aside and grabbed his coffee.

"That one," he said as he pointed to the one in her other hand, "was after a fire at a school. When I came around the corner of the truck and saw you there, standing alone, I clicked the picture with my phone. It struck me…how beautiful you looked right then."

She studied the photo—she was standing in a background of dust and smoke, filthy, in her gear, leaning back against the truck with her eyes closed as if she had to escape for just a minute. Or as if she was too tired to move another step.

"Beautiful? I'm dirty and in bulky firefighting gear."

Even so, she examined the picture, intrigued. So this is what she'd done. This is what she'd looked like doing it.

"You helped save twenty-seven kids that day. They were all trapped in a science lab at the back of the school, and one little girl wouldn't come to any of us.

She was too frightened. But she came to you. It was a long, hard day, but a good one. I could see it all in your face, in your posture. How much heart you have. How much you had to hold back to keep a clear head and help them."

Erin swallowed hard, her eyes burning. She put the pictures down, overcome with emotion. If this was everything she'd been, what she'd had—she'd also lost all of it. The pain of it was unbelievable.

"You always liked this," Bo said softly.

He held up a strange turtle with a bobble head that had "I 'Heart' the Bahamas" on its back.

"From the one actual vacation we took together. Some more pictures from the island in there. A few other silly things. A book you bought me for my birthday and a shirt you used to sleep in at my place."

Erin wanted to look, but she also didn't want to. It was almost too much. It had been easier not knowing. Maybe that was a warning—it was a mistake to try to resurrect the past.

"Are you okay?" Bo asked.

She took a breath. "Yes. Sorry. This is a lot. More than I thought it would be."

She picked up the pictures again, sorting through them. The usual array of happy couple photos, always smiling, sometimes romantic and sweet.

It seemed impossible that this couple would have broken up. But they had, apparently.

Bo was quiet as she continued to look, only filling in a detail now and then. Erin kept returning to one picture in particular, of Bo, standing in a room where he stared at the camera very intently. His expression was one of raw hunger, undisguised lust.

"This... I can almost... This is your house. I remember a... I don't know. I can almost see it, but not. Something hanging on the wall behind you, like you are blocking it in the picture?"

She looked at him, expectant.

"There's a small ceramic piece I inherited from my grandmother that you always liked. It was old, antique. From France, I think. You commented on it the first time you came over. That it looked like the garden your father kept when you were a kid."

Erin's eyes widened. "Yes! Yes, it was...oval? And hand-painted?"

Bo nodded, the corner of his gorgeous mouth pulling a slight smile at her excitement. Any doubts or fears that Erin had were washed away in the new memory. She put the pictures down, laughing with glee at yet another part of her past given back to her, and she lunged at Bo, throwing her arms around him.

"Thank you for doing this. For bringing these things over. This is wonderful."

He hugged her back lightly as she squeezed him in her arms, and then realized, as the moment ebbed, that she was almost sprawled completely across him, pressing him back into the cushions.

Her heart raced even faster as she pulled back, but didn't move, looking down into his face.

She dipped down before she could change her mind, kissing him as she wrapped her arms around him again.

He tasted so good. His arms lay at his sides as he let her explore his mouth, let her kiss him. Erin parted his lips, tasted him, went deeper to find more.

This was absolutely the right thing to do.

Angling her body so that she could press her front

to his, she found him hard already and sighed into his mouth.

"This is so good, Bo. How did we ever let this go?"

It was the wrong thing to say.

He stilled beneath her, drawing back to look at her with passion but also…caution. Lifting off him, she sat, unsure what to do with her hands so she picked up the turtle again. Bo sat up, too, taking a minute or two to compose himself, as if he were deciding what to say.

"This will work. I know it. For all the weirdness, I want to do this with you. Please tell me you do, too," she said, hoping against hope that he wasn't going to back away or change his mind again.

His chest expanded as he took a deep breath, released it, and he offered a nod.

"I do. But we need to be clear on what 'this' is. We broke up, Erin, and this isn't a reconciliation. We're not starting again. If this works out the way you want it to, you'll know that. Remember, you wanted out. And at some point, you'll remember why. So let's not fool ourselves or pretend it's anything other than what it is. I care about you or I wouldn't be here—but what happens between us, it's not going anywhere. When it's done, you'll go on with your life, and so will I. You should know, going in, that I'm leaving in August."

That surprised her. "Leaving? Where?"

"I'm taking a job with a federal task force with the FBI. No one knows, so please keep it between us for now. I agree with what you said—I think we need closure. It all ended so fast before. I did some research, and the doctor said it was possible that you could remember if—"

"Wait. What doctor? You told someone about this?"

"Dr. Newcomb. I didn't tell her anything specific. Just in theory, she said being with someone you were in a relationship with could trigger some memories. It might make you feel safe enough to do so. I needed to know that. That this really could help."

"Okay. I guess I can understand that. If that's what you needed to be sure, then okay. And I'm happy for you, about the job. Really. You're right—it's good to get the ground rules out in the open. And I…I like you, too. As much as I know you. I do feel safe with you. I have since I woke up, which was confusing. I thought it was the uniform," she said with a self-effacing chuckle.

Bo smiled, too. "She also said that if you want to see her, she's always happy to make an appointment for you."

Erin shook her head. "I don't need a shrink. I need my life back. I need you." She took a breath, calmed her voice. "I know what we had… Sexually, it had to be good, right?"

"It was mind-bending."

"Wow, okay, no pressure, right?"

"You don't have anything to worry about."

"It's something I haven't talked to anyone about, but Bo, I can't even remember my first time having sex with someone. I don't remember sex with *anyone*. I guess I was a late bloomer. I don't know what I like or don't like, and I can't even remember if I'm any good at it."

His hand came up, touched her cheek lightly. "You're insanely good at it. Believe me."

She smirked. "Well, thanks, except then all of the experience that made me any good is now gone— unless it's like all the other stuff that the doctors said I didn't lose—like driving my car or doing yoga. Maybe sex is like that? I guess being with you is the only way I can know. And when it's over, it's over. When you have to leave, you go. No matter if my memory is back or not. That's a good thing. It gives us a...deadline. But you know, if I'm not any good, and if you don't want to, you have to tell me."

He touched her chin, smiled slightly. "I don't think that will be a problem, but I'll let you know, sure."

It was a strange conversation, this verbal contract they were hammering out, but it was also raising the anticipation. Bo was watching her. Waiting until she was done. He shifted his position, sitting up straighter.

"Likewise, I want you to be very honest with me about what you want or don't want. I'll show you what we liked, what we did...but if you don't want that now, it's okay. Just say so."

Her heart was beating fast in her chest, her mind racing as she wondered what delicious, kinky things they might have done.

"Were there ever...other people?" She wasn't sure why she asked, but something tickled at the back of her brain, that she and Bo might not have been very vanilla in their sex lives.

"No. Never that. Only us. I don't like to share."

She let out a breath of relief. "Good. Me, either. At least, I don't think so. So that means, um, we're exclusive for this time, too, right? You're not seeing anyone else right now?"

"I haven't seen or been with another woman since we broke up."

That surprised her, but she didn't say so.

"So yes, we're exclusive for now. Are you still on birth control?"

"Yes." The conversation was so...calm, so business-like, but all the same, her blood was rushing to every spot that it needed to and a few extra.

She wanted him. As they sat there talking, she could barely hold back from touching him.

"I haven't been with anyone else, but if you want me to use protection, I will. We never did, not after the first month together."

She considered that for a few minutes. If he were a stranger, she'd never go for it, of course. She thought about that photo on the beach. Bo wouldn't lie to her. Not about this.

"I don't know if I was with anyone else."

The flicker of pain in his face made her immediately regret the disclosure. "But I had every test imaginable when I was hospitalized, and I'm completely healthy. Well, except for the memory loss."

He reached over and cupped a hand around her jaw. Bo stared into her eyes so hard, she couldn't say anything else. That was okay; the expression on his face told her that they were done talking.

Bo saw the flush move up Erin's throat. She'd been getting aroused simply by talking about their agreement. But this was more than he expected, too. Though he should have considered it, he hadn't considered that Erin had no memory of sex whatsoever. She wasn't a virgin, physically, but if she couldn't remember ever having sex...wasn't that almost the same thing?

This was about more than trying to trigger a few memories. It was about making some new ones for her, whether he'd thought of that or not. But here he was, and he wanted her. Desperately.

"What do you want me to do?" she asked, sitting across from him, her hands in her lap.

He lounged back, throwing one arm over the back of the sofa, open to her.

"What do you want, Erin?"

She scooted closer, her thighs pushing up against his. "I want to kiss you."

Bo was hard again, but he was going to let her set the pace if it killed him.

He remembered his first time, which was also the first time for the girl he had been with, too. They'd kissed a lot, fumbled a lot and had fun. It hadn't mattered that neither of them really knew what they were doing, and he'd been fifteen, so there was no way he could have.

But now it mattered, though he also knew a lot more, and wanted to make this good for her. Memorable.

Erin licked her lower lip, looking slightly unsure, and he shifted so that he could slide his arm behind her, pulling her up close.

"A good old-fashioned make-out session, then?" he said with a smile, looking into her eyes.

He didn't wait for her answer as he looped his arm around the back of her neck and pulled her close, trapping her against him as his lips covered hers.

The previous kisses they'd shared at the bar and the diner had been rushed and hungry. They had time now. Nowhere to be; no need to hurry. So he didn't. Bo took his time, exploring every angle of her mouth, starting with light, teasing kisses that she returned enthusiastically as he gradually deepened his exploration.

She was so damned sweet. He hadn't spent this much time kissing anyone—only kissing—in a very long time. He and Erin had enjoyed kissing, but it was usually an accompaniment to what else they were doing. Only new couples ever sat and kissed like this, and it made him realize they never really had. Their first time had been hot and insane, in the truck outside the diner. They'd skipped this sweet-hot buildup. The slow part. It was intoxicating.

Though he wasn't sure how much he could take when she turned the tables, pushing him back on the sofa and crawling over his lap to straddle him. Still, they continued only to kiss, though the heat was climbing as the kisses became more carnal. Wetter, deeper... their tongues doing what he wanted to do to her elsewhere.

She moaned against him, pressing her breasts to his chest, and shifting to grind herself against the ridge in his jeans.

Erin may have forgotten her sex life, but she remembered how to move her body all too well. He was too hot, too ready for her to keep doing that without him losing it.

She was in the same condition, if the quick little panting sounds she made into his neck as she nipped him there meant anything.

He put his hands on her hips, held her still.

"Two more minutes of that, honey, and this will be all over with," he said hoarsely, wishing he had more control. But it had been a long time, and this was every fantasy that had kept him awake for months coming true.

She leaned her forehead against his. "Sorry, I need… you, Bo. Now."

5

ERIN COULD HAVE cried with joy and relief as Bo met her eyes, his gaze warm.

"I need you, too."

Until now, she thought it might not really happen. She waited, but he didn't do anything. Then she realized he was waiting.

For her.

"I really am ready, Bo."

He relaxed a bit and reached for her. "I think getting these clothes off would be a good start, then."

She smiled as she bent down to drag her lips along his jaw, over to his mouth where she tasted him again for long, starving minutes, as if she hadn't just kissed him for a full half hour straight.

She began to pull her shirt off, but he stood and stopped her.

"Not here. Upstairs."

A part of her didn't want to stop—what if one of them had second thoughts? What if they lost the mood? She left her doubts unspoken as she led him up the stairs.

Her room was as plain and boring as the rest of the house, but he didn't seem to care. She headed to the bed, but he guided her gently to the other side of the room, instead. In front of the large mirror on the wall.

Then he reached around her from behind and started undoing the buttons of her blouse, both of them watching.

Erin thought her knees might give out as the heels of his hands rubbed on her nipples while he undid those buttons. She was so glad she'd opted for no bra.

He left the blouse on, letting it fall open as he slid his hands up over her ribs and then over her breasts as he kissed her neck.

"Bo, please." She sighed. She wasn't even sure what she was begging for as her head fell back against him, the sensations of his kissing and his rough hands massaging her breasts and thrumming her nipples nearly undid her right there.

"Please what?"

She shook her head, reaching back to find his hardness and closing her hand over him the best she could. He moved away, and she bit out a sound of objection.

"More. I need more of you. I need…more."

"Okay," he said agreeably as he continued to tease her. His hands drifted from her breasts to the snap on her jeans, which he undid. She shimmied out of her jeans and kicked them to the side. Bo looked at her over her shoulder.

"See how beautiful you are? You make me crazy. I want to plant your hands on that mirror and watch so that you can see what we do to each other."

Erin could hardly breathe. She wanted that so much.

His being dressed made her feel exposed. Vulnerable. In a good way, though.

He pulled her close, started kissing her forehead, her cheeks, her lips...then her neck, shoulders, and he just kept going.

He stayed awhile at her breasts, kissing her there until she was winding her fingers through his hair to steady herself. Then, down her stomach he went, until he was on his knees in front of her.

She couldn't take her eyes off the sight in the mirror. Bo before her, lifting her knee. He dipped his tongue in to touch her, making her cry out harshly, her hands clinging to his shoulders.

She couldn't say anything but his name, the warm, soft, rhythm of his tongue making her move against him until she was coming apart, sensation making her seek more, beg for more.

He gave it to her. Erin was barely standing now as he wrung every last whimper from her body.

When her cries of pleasure ebbed to shuddering breaths, he moved away, but was careful to make sure she was okay. When he looked up at her, Erin was struck by the raw emotion and passion in his expression, nothing hid from her.

"You're still dressed." Her voice didn't even sound like her own.

He stood, waiting. She reached forward with shaking hands, sliding them up under the T-shirt and reveling in every rippled muscle she felt there. He raised his arms, threw the shirt to the side as she worked his belt, his jeans, until those were gone, too.

Then all she could do was stare.

She was glad she couldn't remember anyone else.

If she never saw another man in her life, she couldn't imagine one that would be more perfect, more masculine, than Bo.

His cock jutted out at her, hard and eager. She closed her hand around him, felt that skin-to-skin contact for the first time.

He cursed under his breath, his body tense as stone, but his expression told her everything she needed to know. She was moved by the need and the honesty in his face. Without him asking, she faced the mirror, placed her hands on it. Met his eyes where he watched from behind her. He joined her, widening her stance gently and pulling her hips up to meet him.

Erin bit her lip as he nudged her, slid forward, rubbing over her sensitized skin, making her gasp.

No way would she have thought she was ready again, but her body felt otherwise.

She arched her back, trembling in anticipation.

"Oh, Erin…." The words ground out of him as he thrust inside, filling her completely. "Sorry…I meant to go slower."

He was breathing so hard, his face tight, eyes burning. She met his gaze in the mirror and shook her head.

"Don't. Don't go slow. Take what you need. Give me what I need."

None of this generated anything in her memory, but her body knew him—knew him well. She also knew how to move to please him. How to plant her feet, how to roll her hips in a manner that made him emit a guttural moan and swell even larger.

She couldn't imagine how she might remember anything, as she couldn't even think—the tightening in her body wiped everything away but the pleasure. Her response sparked his until he called her name out, too, the gut-wrenching tenderness and relief in his tone touching something deep inside her as he rode out his own climax.

As everything slowed and calmed she turned and went into his arms as if it were the most natural thing in the world to do. They stayed wrapped together like that until their breathing settled, the heat easing.

"That was…amazing."

She felt his chest shake as he chuckled and dropped a kiss on her hair.

"Yeah, it was."

"Was it always like that with us?"

"It wasn't always the same, but it was always good, yes. Did anything seem familiar?"

Oddly, she didn't want to go there. Didn't want to interrupt this moment with the past. She shook her head.

"No, though you felt…familiar. Like I knew what to do with you."

"That's a start."

"Do you want a shower?"

"I could use one. You want to go first?"

"There's room for two," she said, not wanting to be separate from him yet.

Remember what this is, she cautioned herself.

She knew. She did. Eyes wide-open.

Erin knew what they were doing, but that didn't mean she wouldn't feel things for him. She might feel quite a lot.

"Why don't you rest up for a while? Maybe we can get some dinner or something later," he suggested.

Hint taken. He needed some distance, and it was the least she could do.

This had to be harder for him, maintaining the emotional boundaries, given their past. She had, after all, left him. Forgotten him. He wasn't packing up and leaving, he simply wanted to shower alone. He'd be there later when she woke up.

She forced a smile. "I could use a nap."

He leaned over, kissed her cheek, then her lips.

"I'll wake you up in a bit."

There was sensual promise in his voice that made it a lot better. She watched him walk out of the bedroom. Her body chilled in the absence of his heat. She pulled the thick quilt up and over her body, still so sensitive from his touch.

Maybe this was going to be more difficult than she thought, she pondered as her eyes slipped shut. She heard the shower come on down the hall, comforting her that Bo was still there as she drifted off and let it all go for a while.

Bo STOOD IN the shower under the scalding water, wondering if he was losing his mind.

The sex had been every bit as powerful as he remembered, and then some. It hadn't affected Erin's memory, but it sure had triggered his. Being with her was dangerous. He had thought he could do this, but now he wasn't sure.

Yet how could he walk away? What kind of man would say, "Sorry, this isn't going to work," after what he'd done with her?

He scrubbed up and got out, grabbing a towel that hung on the back of the door. It smelled like her. That brought back memories, too. They would always shower together under the guise of saving time, but it never did. They ran out of hot water almost every time.

The only way he could manage this was to make it about the sex. He would wear himself out with her, use her, let her use him, in any way they both needed, and then it would be over. Hell, it was over before it started.

He wrapped the towel around himself and went back down to Erin's room. He should have brought his clothes out with him. He didn't want to disturb her.

It would have also made it easier to leave. To get some space. Send a clear message that this was about sex, not a relationship. Nothing more than helping her with her problem, and hopefully getting her out of his system.

Or, he could do what he said he would. Wake her up, roll around with her in that big bed for a while, and then go get some food.

He blew out a breath, unsure what he was going to do, but knowing he couldn't just leave. He'd agreed to help her, and it wasn't her fault if he was feeling jumpy about the whole thing now.

Going past the bed to where he'd thrown his clothes over the back of a chair, he stopped, making the mistake of watching her sleep. He'd done that a lot before, since she could drop off to sleep with no effort at all, and be snoring without him even closing his eyes.

Then her hair would be tangled, spilled all over the pillow. Now it was too short for that, but mussed from his hands nonetheless. She'd pulled the quilt over her, one delicate shoulder exposed, tempting him.

He could crawl in there with her. Wake her up the way he did so often before. Erin always loved sleepy sex.

Once hadn't been near enough to sate the need she'd

rekindled earlier. He dropped the towel, crawled in under the quilt with her.

Her eyes opened as soon as he did, startled at first, drawing back and then relaxing.

"Sorry. I'm not used to anyone being in bed with me."

He smiled, but the words only emphasized that for all of the times together that he could remember, she only remembered what happened today.

"Let me go clean up, too, and then—"

"Not yet," he said, nibbling her shoulder, already hard for her.

"But I'm—"

He cut off their conversation with a kiss, quickly rolling her onto her back and covering her completely. Her arms came around him, and she arched up into him, clearly on the same page.

"Was it always like this? Like we couldn't get enough?" she asked breathlessly, stroking his back.

"Especially at first, yeah. Pretty much all we did was have sex," he said with a laugh, looking down into her face.

"I find that easy to believe."

She pushed on his chest, rolling him onto his back as she came over him and took him deep, as if she couldn't wait. The eagerness and desire in her face satisfied him as nothing else ever had. Erin had always been good in bed, but she'd never been this open with him. She liked to be in control, and he didn't mind that one bit, except that it had always put distance between them.

There was no distance now as she rocked her hips, scraping her nails over his chest and making him share some pretty graphic thoughts with her as she did so.

"Come here." He tugged on her hand until she collapsed over him, seeking his kiss, but he went lower, sucking her nipples, making her frantic as she rode him.

Causing Erin to lose control was the most erotic thing he'd ever experienced, chanting his name and pulling him along with her on the current. When they were done, they showered again, and ran out the hot water.

Bo was exhausted when they made their way back to the bed, falling into it, and he curled around her. He hadn't been sleeping long when he heard his beeper, buzzing on the dresser.

"I have to check that."

He slid from the warm cocoon of her body and grabbed his phone, calling in.

"What's wrong?"

Erin pushed up on one elbow, the blanket slipping down to reveal her breasts. Bo swallowed hard, trying not to look. She was so hot, and all he wanted was to go back to bed and ignore the rest of the world.

"They need me at a fire. I have to go."

"Now?"

"Yes, I'm afraid so."

"Can I come with you?"

"I don't think it's a good idea. I need to close everything else out when I'm there, and I don't think I can do that when you're around. Especially looking like that."

She took a second as if to absorb the information and nodded, blowing him a kiss.

"Okay. Make sure you come back."

Bo stood transfixed for a second as she relaxed into the pillows. It was like going back in time. She might not remember, but that was what they both said when they went to work. Never goodbye. Always "Make sure you come back." Because they knew that in their profession, there was always a chance they wouldn't.

He kissed her quickly and then tore himself from the room, hurrying down to his truck.

Fifteen minutes later, he approached the scene, showing his badge as he made his way past the barricade at the end of the street. His mind clicked over to work.

It was a bad one. Three structures, at least. Several stations were on hand, and a few volunteer units. He counted two ambulances, and then saw the coroner's van just past them.

"Damn," he bit out under his breath, grabbing his stuff and exiting the truck, making notes as soon as he did. They were still putting out the fire. It would be hours, perhaps days, before he could get inside to do a real assessment. But the chief met him out near the street.

"Myers. Glad you're here."

"What can I do? I can't investigate yet."

"Won't be sure until you take a look, but from what we can tell, it started at four to six different points, simultaneously."

"A timer and a fuse, all set to ignite at the same time?"

"Yep. Seems like the same guy who set the fire on Riley and Joe."

"It's been a while. And this one is bigger. Residences, not a warehouse. So that's different. Casualties?"

"One. Three of our guys hurt, but they'll be okay.

Weird accidents again—Mitchell said he fell through
the floor when all of it was solid, and then there was
a spot where it busted through, but he saw it too late.
It's like the place was booby-trapped for them when
they went in. Accidents happen, but not this many, not
all at once. Something's off."

Bo felt a chill settle at the base of his spine.

Is that what had happened to Erin and Joe? Had it
been a trap?

"So we might have some maniac rigging fires to
lure us in, and then he sets up traps inside the buildings? Makes it look like an accident."

The chief was grim. "I'll get you in as soon as I
can. You can talk to my guys as soon as medical clears
them."

"Thanks. Let me know any further developments."

The chief went back to his team, and Bo stayed to
watch, studying the fire and the crowd, taking notes.
He'd head to the hospital after this, talk to the men who
were hurt. See what they could remember.

If they had a serial arsonist on their hands—and one
who was targeting firefighters—this was a much bigger problem than he'd anticipated. And Erin's memory
of events could be even more important than she knew.

He couldn't leave the scene now; he was going to
need to talk to anyone who'd witnessed the event, get
pictures gawkers might have taken with their phones,
or ones from traffic and security cameras. He'd start
amassing information that he'd add to the case file in
his office.

Bo focused on his work, and that's all that consumed
his attention. It was a relief of sorts.

Here, he knew what he was doing. He was, as much

as he could be, in control of the situation. He knew what to ask, what to do, and he was very good at it. Confusion was behind him, with Erin, and for now, he left it there.

6

KIT WAS HAVING a bad morning, and that was an understatement.

Erin was remaining tight-lipped and distant, stewing in her own amnesiac juices. She'd been like that for the past few days. She'd come in for the morning and worked on abusing more plants before she lit out with barely a goodbye. Something was going on, but Erin wasn't about to tell Kit what. In addition, her other part-timer hadn't shown up today, having had to go to the hospital because her daughter had their second grandchild.

The bell rang as her next appointment arrived. After spending two hours with an almost-impossible-to-please bride whom Kit had finally managed to quell—while handling the counter—she took a breather. Luckily, that wedding account alone would keep her afloat for another month.

Kit sighed, gathering up the flowers that Erin had savaged earlier in the day. Before she could try to redo the arrangements, her cell rang.

"Hey, Kit."

"Walt. What's up?" It was her delivery guy.

"I'm stranded. Something in the engine blew on the van, and I'm out past Baldwinsville. I called for a tow, but they're not here yet."

"Are you okay?"

"Yeah, I'm fine, but there's no way I'll get all these deliveries done today."

Kit closed her eyes. She had known she needed a new van for some time. Money, of course, was the issue. And there'd be no money if those flowers didn't get delivered.

She heard the bell out front and pulled her shoulders up straight. No one said running a small business was easy. She'd have to try to catch Erin, and if possible, have her pick up the flowers for delivery. That could save the day.

"Thanks, Walt. Go with the van and see what the repairs are—take it to Ike's, and I'm going to try to contact Erin to come by and grab the remaining deliveries. Tell the garage not to make any repairs until I know exactly how much they'll cost."

"Will do, Kit. I'll let you know."

Kit hung up the phone and went out to the front. The first thing she saw was a large, strong male back. The man leaned down to smell a bouquet of Gerbera daisies. As she caught his profile, she knew exactly who it was.

"Hank?"

He spun abruptly, nearly upsetting the vase of flowers, but he was quick and caught it before it fell.

"Hey, Kit. How are ya?"

She swallowed hard, raising a hand to smooth her hair and wishing she wasn't wearing her work apron. She'd had a fantastic time with Hank the other night, dancing the whole evening away. He'd walked her to her car and kissed her until her toes curled before he said good-night.

He hadn't asked or pushed for anything more than the kiss, and she'd been awake for hours, like a teen-age girl, thinking about it.

"What are you doing here?"

"I thought you might like to get some dinner. You know, with me. I'm on my three-day-off rotation."

"Oh, I really can't. I'm alone here today, and my driver just called. The van broke down, and I have to try to get a hold of Erin to see if she can be there in time to pick up the remainder and get them delivered, or I have to close and go get them myself."

She hated to close, but the flowers that needed delivering were money in the bank, and she probably wouldn't have much more walk-in traffic today.

Hank stepped up close, reaching out to take one of her curls and rubbing it between his fingers. Then he slid his hand behind her neck before he lowered to capture her lips in a kiss.

For one beautiful second, Kit forgot everything— the flowers, the van, Erin and all her troubles—as Hank's mouth worked some magic on hers. He pulled her up tight against him, and there was no mistaking that the kiss was working on him, too.

When he broke away, they were both breathless.

"Sorry, Kath, but I've been thinking about nothing else but kissing you again since the other night."

Kit was wordless. He was the only one who ever called her anything but Kit and she liked it. But she also didn't have time for it.

"I had a lot of fun the other night, but I don't have time for this right now."

He watched her closely, and his friendly gaze took on a special, masculine warmth as it traveled over her face.

"What can I do to help?"

"Huh?"

"You're having a tough day. How can I help?"

Kit was taken off guard. If she couldn't name the last time someone had made her toes curl, she really couldn't remember when someone had asked to help, and out of the blue.

"Oh, that's not necessary."

"C'mon, Kath," he said softly, turning her around as his strong hands rubbed her neck in a heavenly way that made it hard to think. "You have a lot of fires to put out today, and guess what? That's what I do. I put out fires."

She smiled. "You're good at starting them, too, I'd say."

She was flirting. She couldn't resist.

Hank chuckled. "Where is Erin?"

"She left earlier, but I can try her cell. Hopefully she has it on, though she was in a mood earlier, so probably not."

She grabbed her phone. Hank stopped her.

"Let her be. I'll do it."

"What?"

"Tell me where to go, what to do, and I can get your deliveries done."

She turned back around, facing Hank, and couldn't help but be skeptical. "Are you joking?"

"Nope. I've never delivered flowers, but I did a stint

delivering pizzas in college. How different can it be? Give me the rundown, and I'll go finish your deliveries. I can do tomorrow, too, if you need me to. My SUV should handle whatever you've got."

"You must have better things to do on your days off."

"Not really. I coach peewee baseball, but that's not until tomorrow night."

Kit wasn't sure what to say. She liked Hank, she truly did—and she could fall for him. It would be easy enough. But she didn't want to do that. He might be charming and attentive now, but his heart belonged to his job.

But she also needed her flowers delivered.

"Is this your way of angling for a date?"

"No. I thought that was a given."

When he smiled like that, she lost track of everything. But what he was offering was better than sex— well, almost.

"Okay. Yes, thank you. I'd appreciate it. And it's not complicated. Just a few basic rules."

"Tell me what you need me to do, and I'll do my best to give you exactly what you need."

He had that mischievous look in his eye again, and Kit felt it warm parts of her body that should know better. She blinked, snapping out of her minifantasy.

"Um, here, let me give you copies of the delivery sheets just in case, and you can get the rest from Walt. He'll be at Ike's Garage. You know where that is?"

"I do."

Kit busied herself getting the materials together for Hank, and then called Walt to let him know about the change.

"Okay, he's on his way to Ike's now. You can meet him there."

"Will do."

Hank headed for the door.

"Hank," she called, stopping him. "Thank you. I owe you for this."

The look in his eye set her day right again.

"I'll keep that in mind, honey. See you later."

ERIN HAD EVERY intention of driving home. Instead, she found herself at the home improvement store a few miles from her house, where she was spending too much money and fiercely concentrating on paint colors and new bathroom tile. It kept her from going crazy thinking about Bo.

Two days.

It had been two days since he'd had sex with her and then left her hanging. Maybe he'd gotten everything that he wanted. Maybe she'd not been what he wanted or—her secret fear—maybe she hadn't been any good. His response to her seemed to contradict that, but maybe he'd even been lying about going to a fire. Maybe he'd needed to get out. Maybe he'd just wanted to have sex with her one more time before he left her, evening out the score.

The last part, she knew, was her imagination throwing darts at her. Bo wasn't like that—she didn't think so anyway.

But he hadn't come back and he hadn't called.

She had too much pride to chase him, so instead, she discussed the combination of earth tones and brighter colors for her first-floor rooms, the lighting, and how it would all work together.

Then she carted it all home, spread drop cloths everywhere and started to work. There seemed to be so few things she could control in her life, but the color of her walls was one that she could.

Thankfully, since she'd never really hung anything on the walls, they didn't need any fixing or repair, and they were already painted the dull beige, so she didn't need to prime. She was good to go, and the tension that had been dogging her began to ease as she rolled on a nice cinnamon-brown that reminded her of Bo's eyes.

Cursing, she wrenched the roller away from the wall and ended up splattering paint down the front of herself, including on her face.

Safety glasses hadn't seemed necessary for painting, but good thing she'd worn them anyway.

Sighing, she sat down on the plastic-covered floor, using a rag to wipe some of the splatter off. As she looked at the huge array of paint cans she'd brought home among the other various supplies, her head dropped into her hands.

What had she done?

She wasn't sure the question was about the paint binge—not completely.

Just then, the doorbell rang, and she popped to her feet, peering out the window before she opened it. She wasn't expecting anyone.

Bo.

She seriously considered not answering the door, but he'd seen her look from the window and offered a short wave.

Pulling open the door, she stood in the open space rather than inviting him in.

"Hi." His smile was warm. Sexy.

Sure it was.

"Hi."

Long. Awkward. Pause.

"Um, can I come in?

"Sure."

He stepped inside, moving past her. Normally, a guy might kiss his girl hello when he showed up at her house, but they weren't like that, were they?

"Painting?"

He took in the supplies and drop cloths with a raised eyebrow.

"Yeah. I thought it was time to personalize the place a bit."

He checked out her face and her clothes, visually tracing the cinnamon-brown streak from cheek to thigh.

"The paint fights back?"

She smiled stiffly and crossed her arms in front of her. "Why are you here?"

He blinked, looking slightly taken aback by her abruptness.

"To see you. And also to see if you had time to go somewhere with me."

A date?

"Where?"

"A fire site. I'd like you to look at it with me."

Okay, so not a date.

"Why?"

"I'd rather not get into details, but do you have time?"

He looked at the paint again.

"I have to clean up."

His gaze followed her curiously but he didn't stop

her as she stepped around him, heading for the stairs. She didn't want to acknowledge the disappointment that he hadn't come here to see her. It was only business.

She put it aside and took a quick shower, washing the paint off and putting on clean jeans and a shirt. She didn't worry about what she threw on, as it obviously didn't matter.

When she returned downstairs, not more than a half hour later, the entire wall she'd been working on was painted. A first coat anyway. Bo was sealing up the paint can.

He didn't have a speck of cinnamon-brown on him.

"You finished it."

"There wasn't much left to do on this wall. Nice choice of color. Warms up the room. There are enough windows in here so it doesn't darken it down too much."

"Thanks, I liked it, too." She felt stupidly pleased that he approved of her color of paint. "I'm ready if you are."

"Are you okay?"

He stood in front of her, blocking her route to the door.

"Sure, why?"

"You're not making eye contact, and you're being very...cool. Even for you."

Erin blinked. Even for her? What did *that* mean?

She put her hands on her hips and looked him fully in the face, making sure she made *total* eye contact.

"Yes, as a matter of fact, I was wondering why we had this big talk three days ago, then you slept with me and ignored me ever since. You haven't even picked up the phone." She shook her head, disgusted. "Other than that, nothing's wrong at all."

He actually had the gall to look mildly surprised. Maybe more so at her frankness, but Erin wasn't in the mood to be coy.

"I've been at the office or at the fire site for the past few days and most of the evenings. I... You never would have noticed before. You knew about the work. It was never a question when one of us was working. There were no expectations. And now... I just, well, I didn't even think about it." He shook his head, still seeming perplexed. "I'm sorry about that. I got into the job, and I didn't think."

Erin was unsettled at how quickly her anger dissipated, confusion and anxiety taking its place. She didn't know what to think because he knew the rules, and she didn't. She'd thought they'd fight, but that was what couples did. And they weren't a couple—not really.

"You're right. I have no claim on you that way. You don't have to explain anything to me. It was just... confusing."

He came up behind her, put his hands on her shoulders and pulled her back against him. She still held herself stiffly, though, as much as she wanted to curl into his warmth.

"I'm sorry, Erin. I got to the site, and work took over. It's like that. I have to immerse myself in it to do the job well. But I should have called, at least. Though to be honest, I didn't think you'd care."

"I don't. I mean, I cared, but for all the wrong reasons. I feel so stupid. I thought it was me. That you were avoiding me, or that you changed your mind."

"No way. I'm sorry you thought that," he said as his arms came around her in a tight squeeze.

She was embarrassed that her eyes stung as he held her. His body was solid and safe, and Erin accepted the comfort. Needed it.

That probably wasn't a good thing, but it was what it was.

"This sucks. I hate feeling this way."

"How?"

"I don't even know myself. I think, if I could remember, I'd really be angry at myself for being this needy. I don't think I was like that."

"No, you weren't. Ever."

The way he said it sounded like there was more there.

"I had to have needed *you*."

"I think you did, in some ways."

Again, a note of ambiguity in his response, but Erin didn't know if she had the right to push for more.

"But I would never have called you needy," Bo continued. "And you aren't now. Or, if you are, it's understandable," he said, turning her back around to face him.

As if to prove his point, he dipped down and kissed her. Erin clung to him, letting him in, all of her doubt washed away as he stoked the heat inside her quite effectively.

Then he slowed and stopped. "Anyway, as good as it was the other night, I was thinking that what could be more effective for helping your memory would be revisiting some of the things we did, places we went, that kind of thing."

"Like reliving my past?"

"I guess you could look at it that way. I think you can remember, Erin. You've already had some things come back and the rest has to be there waiting under the surface. I think we really can do this, and I'm willing to do whatever it takes."

Erin stepped back, considering him more closely. She was heartened by his apparent commitment to help her, but her gut told her that there was more going on. Studying him, she started to notice the bleariness in his eyes and the shadows underneath. He looked as if he hadn't shaved for at least a day. He'd obviously been working hard while she was wrapped up in her own self-indulgent worries.

"This fire you were at…it was bad?"

He pulled himself up, looking away as he answered. "Yeah, it was."

"Let me get you a beer, and you can tell me about it."

He hesitated, as if apprehensive.

"What's wrong?"

"It would be easy, Erin, to lose track of what this is between us. To forget that we aren't together. We used to do that a lot, sit down and talk over the day, what happened at a fire or at the station. It's hard to know where to draw the lines."

She paused, trying to understand. This had to be hard for him. She let out a heavy breath.

"I know. But I think we need to be all-in, right? We need to act like we are together, like it was, if this is even going to work. But I also know that's asking a lot, and if you want out, I can see why. I've been selfish, only thinking of myself."

It was difficult for her to say, because she wanted this more than anything—to get her memory back. But some part of her railed at causing him any more pain. She couldn't continue to do that in good conscience. She had to at least offer him an out—though she hoped he wouldn't take it.

"No, I don't want out. This is bigger than either of us, really. I need you to remember, too. And you're right. We do need to be all-in. We'll deal with the end of it when we have to."

Erin frowned as she sat down in the chair near her, at the dining-room table, such as it was. Running her hand over the cheap laminate top, the thought of changing it threaded through her mind as Bo sat, too.

"What do you mean that it's bigger than either of us?"

"Listen, why don't we go somewhere to talk? We can skip going to the fire site—it's getting late anyway. Want to head over to the park?"

"Sure, that sounds good."

As they walked out to the truck, her mind revolved around the emerging image of who she was before. Someone who didn't seem to connect with others very well, it seemed. She clearly hadn't been there for her sister, and she'd even kept her lover at a distance—or at least, she'd kept him a secret. All so that she could save face in her work?

A lot of the guys were married or involved, so why had she needed to keep her personal life a secret? Bo had admitted it could be different for women in the department, but…something didn't ring true.

The idea was an uncomfortable one. It circled around in her mind as they drove. She stared out the window, trying to clear her head. There must have been reasons for her being so emotionally unavailable.

If only she could remember them. It was like seeing only half of a picture, other people's impressions, and not being able to see the whole.

They stopped across the street from Dinosaur Bar-B-Que, a Syracuse landmark. The place was hopping.

"I need something to eat. I'll be right back," Bo said and was out the door before she could get her seat belt off to join him.

The man was definitely antsy. Or maybe he was simply hungry.

She watched him jog to the restaurant and saw several women who stood by a line of parked motorcycles watch him, as well—he was impressive in his uniform. And out of it.

He emerged ten minutes later with a bag under either arm, and Erin wondered exactly how much food he'd ordered. Still, when he opened the backseat and put the bags in, the aromas made her mouth water.

"I hope you're hungry," he said with a grin as his eyes met hers.

Her mind went right to the gutter. She was definitely hungry.

Bo got them back out on the highway and before she knew it, they were pulling into the Green Lakes State Park. They carried their bags over to an available picnic table near the lake. Some families were also eating out, though it was a weeknight, but it wasn't too crowded this early in the season.

"I come here to run sometimes, though it's a bit of a drive from my house. But the lakes are so pretty. I can never get over how still they are, and the green-blue color, though I know it's reflecting sediment in the water," she commented as she helped him get the food out of the bags.

"You say that every time we come here," he said absently with a smile, surveying the table.

"Do I give you the lecture on how they are meromictic, probably formed by plunge waterfalls fifteen thousand years ago when the glaciers came through here?"

"Not if I say it first."

She laughed. "We're such geeks."

The food looked great and she began eating, the fresh air making her hungrier than she expected.

"This is such a treat. Thank you. We did this kind of thing often?"

"Yeah, in the warm weather. It reduced the risk of someone seeing us out together."

Erin's easy mood crashed, and she set the juicy rib down that she'd started munching on.

"Was it always like that? Sneaking around and trying to avoid everyone?"

"I told you why. You had your reasons."

"You didn't like it."

"I understood. Especially when we both worked in the station. When I moved out into investigation, I hoped we could be more open, but—"

"That's when things fell apart," she finished. "I can't remember it, but I feel like I need to apologize for it."

"Don't," he said, leveling a look at her. "Let's just enjoy the evening."

She nodded, though her appetite diminished somewhat. His did not, and she realized he probably hadn't had a decent meal in days, either. Was he always this consumed by his work? In relative quiet, they finished their meal as the sun started lowering behind the trees that surrounded the lake.

"So tell me about the fire. What happened?"

He finally relented. "It was a bad one. Three houses, several families with nowhere to go now, and two dead by the time it was done. One of them a teenage mother who must have gotten trapped. Luckily, the baby was elsewhere with her grandmother. Another older man died of smoke inhalation later at the hospital, and four firefighters were injured, though not critically."

"That's tragic," she said, reaching over to put a hand on his arm. He paused and covered her hand with his.

"There's more. The signatures of the fire resemble the ones from some previous incidents."

"So it wasn't an accident?" Suddenly her hands turned cold.

"No. And the evidence so far very closely resembles the methods used in the fire that hurt you and killed Joe—the location is completely different, but we're beginning to suspect the buildings were booby-trapped to injure firefighters going inside."

Erin covered her mouth in shock, astounded. "Oh, no...someone did this on purpose? To target firefighters? And that could have been what happened to me and Joe, too?"

He was tense again, his face drawn into tight, tired lines. "Maybe. Though your fire completely demolished the building so there's not enough evidence to make sure—this time, we had reports from the guys who were hurt and more evidence of the tampering."

She drew her hand back and closed her eyes for a second, digesting that someone had actually planned this. That they had been targeting firefighters and had killed her colleague while nearly killing her.

"So that's what you meant about my remembering being about more than us. I might know something that could stop this."

"Or that could shed light on it, yes. We don't have much to work with, and there are enough differences between the two fires that perhaps they aren't the result of the same arsonist—and if you know that what happened to you was different, that changes things, too. Or you might know something that could help us catch a serial arsonist. A killer."

Erin reeled, standing up from the table and starting to pace, her hands shaking. If she'd felt pressure to remember before, now it was tenfold. Hundredfold.

She was lost in her own panicked thoughts when Bo interrupted her pacing, stopping her in place.

"What if I can't remember? What if nothing happens and more people are hurt?"

Bo shook his head resolutely. "There's no guarantee your case is connected, or that you could remember anything that would help. It's just a chance. I didn't know if I should tell you—the pressure might hold you back."

"Maybe it will, but it also makes me want to try even harder. I want you to tell me everything. We used to talk about work a lot, right? So we'll do that. Tell me everything about the fire."

Bo's mouth flattened as he looked down into her face. She tipped her chin up, showing him that she was fine—and that she wasn't going to take no for an answer.

He relented. "Okay, but let's go for a walk while we talk. I could use the fresh air."

She agreed, helping him pack up the remains of their meal before they started out on the trail. He was quiet until they got farther along the lake, and then he started telling her all of the awful details. Many that she didn't want to hear, but she listened anyway. Erin was determined to see this through to the end, no matter what. As Bo's hand reached out and clasped hers as they walked, it was good to know she wasn't alone.

7

BO'S MOOD IMPROVED by the minute. Though he always
teased Erin about her fascination with the area's geo-
logic origins, he always marveled at them, too.

He loved how completely smooth and undisturbed
the lakes were. Absolutely mirrorlike on a perfect day,
they were very deep. Ancient sediments, never dis-
turbed through the march of time, measured as much
as five hundred feet under the two hundred feet of
water. Everything changed, but not these lakes, not
very much. It was calming to think about, that some
things stayed the same.

The fresh air and beautiful views around the lake
chased away the nightmares of the past few days.
Nightmares that he didn't really want to share with
Erin, though he had to.

She'd listened, asking good questions that, to him,
provided more evidence that her experience and her
knowledge about firefighting were just below the surface—like the ancient sediment at the bottom of the
lake, buried, little bits floating up to the surface.

They paused at a spot on the east side of the lake

that had a buildup of solid sediments and minerals in the form of a reef or shelf, unfortunately called Dead Man's Point. Bo shook his head. He wasn't exactly sure why, but he was tired of death. It seemed to be everywhere. He didn't want to be reminded of it in this beautiful place.

"Hey, are you okay?"

Erin was standing before him, her voice reflecting her concern.

"I'm more concerned about you."

She seemed lovelier, if that was even possible, in the soft evening light. She was still physically fit, but he could tell where her face and her shape had softened slightly, away from the rigors of department work. It looked good on her.

"Why?"

"I was afraid knowing about the fire would be too much, that it might actually make your memory harder to reach. Dr. Newcomb said you needed to feel safe, not pressured."

She took his hand, squeezed. "No. I'm glad you told me. I needed to know. And you needed to talk about it."

He blinked, realizing that he really did. He and Erin were always each other's confidants. Friends and work-mates before they were lovers, they could share things at the end of the day with each other that civilians would have a harder time understanding.

He hadn't known how much he'd missed that until right now.

"There's one more thing I have to ask you."

Her tone was apprehensive, and Bo knew she was still thinking about the fire.

"What's that?"

"If this is a serial arsonist, and if he or she did set the fire that Joe and I were caught in, wouldn't I be a potential threat? Do you think I could be in danger?"

Bo frowned. That had been the one thing he'd held back from her—he didn't want to cause more anxiety than he already had, but he should have known she'd reason it out. Or was it that she had other reason to ask?

"Has anything happened? Anything specific?"

She shook her head. "No, not really. I mean, when I first came home, I felt like someone was watching me sometimes, but the doctors said that happened sometimes with amnesia. A level of anxiety or paranoia that usually fades in time, and it did. But what if someone *was* watching me?"

Bo didn't like that possibility at all. He tried to approach the subject objectively, like an investigator, not like a man who wanted to hide her away and keep her safe from anything. It was more difficult than he expected. This was Erin, and he instinctively wanted to protect her.

"Well, the cases may not be related, but if they are, you'd pose a definite threat. However, your amnesia is pretty general knowledge now. It was in the paper and so forth. That would mean our arsonist probably knows, too. Since he or she risked setting another fire, I'm assuming you've been dismissed as a threat. But if you feel that again, like someone's watching, or if anything makes you feel like something is wrong, you have to tell me immediately, okay?"

She nodded, her expression relaxing slightly.

"I guess you should stay as close as possible, then. For a lot of reasons."

"You're probably right about that."

Tugging her forward against him, Bo kept hold of her hand and caught her jaw in his other palm, keeping her still as he took his time kissing her, letting the feel of her mouth under his erase all the dark clouds that had been plaguing his thoughts.

Erin had always been the only one who could do that.

The realization was not a comfort, given their current situation. It was too easy to forget that this was not going anywhere. But as she said, they needed to be "all-in" and deal with the fallout later. Bo wasn't sure he had any choice in the matter, as he'd never really been "all-out."

She slipped her hand free and wrapped both arms around his neck, bringing herself in even closer to him. He did the same, so that they were as tightly fused as two people could be, almost. Erin loved to kiss, and she was so good at it...but the shadows were lengthening. They had to get back before the park closed.

"Hey, let's keep going. I want to show you something," he said against her cheek.

She laughed, a kind of low, soft laugh from her belly that was at once humorous and sexy as hell.

"Yeah, I'm sure you do," she added, pressing her hips forward into the hard evidence his desire.

He laughed, too, thankful for her humor as he grabbed hold of her hand again.

"Not that. Not yet anyway." Bo felt reinvigorated, as though his earlier exhaustion had completely gone. "We have to walk a bit farther."

They ambled down the narrow path toward the main beach and the parking lot, but still out of sight of both.

Then Bo stopped and pulled her aside, off into the woods.

"Over here...."

They climbed up to a higher spot where some sun was still filtering through, and a wide ledge sprawled out from beneath an outcropping of boulders.

"Do you have any recollections? Any sparks of memory about this spot?"

She stood, looking around, and peered out over the trees.

"No, not really. It is a gorgeous view, though. I take it we've been up here before?"

"A few times."

"Why?"

He couldn't repress his smile at his own memories of this private little nook. They'd discovered it one day while hiking and joking around. Erin had taken off into the woods, daring him to find her, and they both found this little bit of magic. He never saw any other foot traffic up here and assumed it was more or less undiscovered.

Her eyebrows rose as she read his expression. "Ah. So this was like our own lovers' lane, I take it?"

"Something like that. A nice private spot, but we also had to be very quiet, just in case any other hikers heard us from below."

He was hard again, and suddenly unworried about the hour. Bo could see the change in her mood as well, as her lips parted, her eyes darkening.

"So what did we do here exactly? Can you show me?"

The desire was plain on her face, reflected in her stance as she leaned toward him, and he was relieved.

The emotional dependence he'd felt while sharing his thoughts about the fire wasn't what he wanted, but this—this he definitely wanted. Thinking about sex focused his muddled mind. And they'd had sex here, in this spot, several times. There was one time in particular that came to mind for him.

She went to him, standing before him with her hands at her sides as he backed her up against the still-warm surface of the rock.

"Caught between a rock and a hard—"

He cut her joke off with a passionate kiss, and she melted into him, moaning as the kiss became hotter and deeper.

He broke the kiss, his own breathing uneven.

"Maybe we should play a game," he said. "You always liked games."

He spun them around so that his back was to the boulder and she stood in front of him. He waited, her eyes darkening with excitement as he watched her closely, wondering if she would remember what happened here.

"What kind of games?"

"Remember with hide-and-seek, how you would be hotter or colder when you were getting close to finding someone?"

She nodded.

"Well, maybe you should try to remember what we did here last time, and I can tell you if you are getting hotter or colder as you do…"

She smiled. "All in the name of assisting my memory, of course."

"Of course."

Erin appeared more than willing to play—she did

like games—and stood back for a minute, looking him up and down as if trying to decide where to start. Bo enjoyed how she took her time, her close study.

"Maybe you should sit down against the base of the rock?"

He shook his head. "Colder."

She stepped forward, pushing up on her toes to nibble his neck, letting her hand drift down to the front of his jeans.

"A little warmer," he whispered.

"Only a little?"

He shrugged, but there was a sparkle in her eyes—Erin was having fun—that he hadn't seen in a long time.

"Hmm...no hands then?" she posited.

He didn't indicate whether she was right or wrong, and waited to see what she'd do next.

Slowly, she pushed up his shirt, flicking her tongue over his chest and then down to his navel. Licks of fire danced under his skin as she did so.

"Definitely warmer," he said, his voice hoarser.

She continued her barrage of light kisses, driving him mad, and then she took the additional liberty of freeing his painfully erect shaft as she did so.

"Hotter," he managed, his body tight with anticipation.

Erin lowered to her knees, her hands on his thighs as she tasted him lightly, rolling her tongue around the tip of him, teasing. Bo's mind blanked.

She looked up at him through her lashes. "Hotter?"

Her tone was all sex kitten, making him even harder. "Very."

He put his hand at the back of her head, applying

gentle but firm pressure until his cock brushed the back of her throat and her lips closed around the root.

Her moan told him that she was okay with his touch. Maybe more than okay. Bo took it the next step, curling his fingers into her hair and pulling back gently, showing her the pace he wanted. The world spun as he watched her move against him, and his hold changed to a light caress of her silky locks. As she lost herself in the act, he let go, needing his hands to brace himself against the boulder as she took the lead, making him tremble from head to toe.

Bo stared out at the lakes in the distance as dusk fell; a guttural moan came from his solar plexus as hot pleasure rose. When he couldn't take it anymore, he reached down and drew her up.

The desire and sheer wanton joy in her expression, her reddened lips and hazy eyes nearly did him in.

She read his mind and shucked her jeans, letting him put her back against the rock. She could barely restrain a gasp of pure bliss as he brought her legs up around him and thrust inside.

"So, so hot," he breathed against her skin.

This he could handle. Erin needy against him, her face a study in sex, her eyes focused only on him.

The boulder was unyielding, and suddenly Erin's moaning became a fervent cry of release—which triggered his own. A sensation of complete and utter satisfaction overwhelmed him. He eased off Erin, but slipped his hand into hers, not wanting to break their contact just yet.

By the time they caught their breath, it was almost dark. As she put her clothes back on, they were quiet.

Then she paused and tilted her head, as if trying to hear something.

"What is it?" Bo asked.

She smiled, taking a deep breath before she spoke.

"Last time, it was in the daylight. I remember looking up, when you were inside me, against the rock, and seeing the sun coming down through the trees."

"That's right. It was." He confirmed her memory with a smile, but behind it, a slight sinking sensation returned.

He should have been as thrilled as she seemed to be. But every memory coming back to her brought them that much closer to what had separated them before. Bo went ahead, making sure they got down the darker hillside safely, though he didn't reach for her hand again as they walked back to the truck.

KIT WAS SO tired by the time she pushed the key into the lock of her back door that night she could just about stand. After Hank had saved the day delivering her flowers, the bad luck had continued. A shipment of flowers came in spoiled, and a customer complained, as well, about their delivery being late that day.

Not to mention Erin was MIA and Kit had kind of hoped she might be there when she got home.

To be honest, she was also disappointed about Hank's not coming back to the store after he was done. She had no right to be—he'd saved her butt finishing the deliveries and following up on the van, which was going to be less expensive than she thought to fix. That was one good thing.

He'd checked in and told her he had something else he had to do that evening, but would see her later. She'd been disappointed—very much so. She'd wondered, if he came back to the shop, where that might lead.

Instead, here she stood, alone as usual. She sat down at the small table by the window that looked out over a very ragged garden—if it could even be called that anymore. How ironic was it that she, a professional florist, had such a messy, unkempt garden?

It had been her mother's pride and joy. For a while after she died, Kit had kept it up, but gardening took time.

There was a message blinking on the machine— Erin? She almost never got calls on her landline anymore, except for telemarketers. She'd been meaning to close out the account for a while and just go to cell. But Erin thought it was important to have as a backup for emergencies, and for 911. Ever the firefighter.

Kit hit the button and listened to the pleasant male voice calling to inform her that a letter would soon arrive informing her that she had been chosen for a personal tax audit from the IRS.

She dropped back into the chair, shaking her head. Chosen? Like she'd won a prize?

Great. This was exactly what she needed. There was nothing amiss in her files, and she kept meticulous records, but it was one more thing to worry about. The call went on with more details, but she wandered away from the room.

Whatever.

Sometimes when she got home, she'd watch some TV or read, but tonight she was just going to bed.

The house was so quiet, though. Until she heard footsteps on the front porch, and then a knock at the door.

Startled, she switched on the porch light. The sheer

white curtain obscured the window, but not so much that she couldn't recognize Hank's huge profile.

She smiled and rushed to the door, then felt silly, slowing down and waiting a beat as she opened it.

"Hank. What are you doing here?"

"Hi, Kath. I hope you don't mind me coming by."

"Um, no, not at all. But how did you know where I live?"

"Miraculous thing, the white pages."

Kit laughed, feeling foolish yet again.

"Now I see the definite value in having kept my landline."

He smiled and looked past her into the house. "I wanted to apologize for not coming back to the shop. I had to go over to my sister's to help her with her kid for a while. She's a single mom, so I sometimes babysit at the drop of a hat, but I'm sorry that I left you hanging."

"We didn't have any definite plans."

"No, but there was that date you owed me, and I said I'd see you later. And this is later."

"That's true."

"Do you want to go out?"

"Not really," she said, and saw him frown. "But I could open a bottle of wine or cook something if you want to come in."

"I'd like that a lot."

He stepped inside and waited in the small entryway as she closed the door.

"Nice house. Where you grew up?"

"Yes, thanks. I love living here, though I haven't been able to keep things up as much as I should. It's a big house."

"Your parents left it to you?"

"Yes, well, Erin and I both inherited it, but I'd been living here taking care of my mom when she was sick, and Erin had already bought her own house, so she signed it over to me. She never was as attached to it as I was. So yeah, it's all mine. Every pipe that needs repair, peeling exterior paint, overgrown garden and all."

"Hey, you're only one person, and you run your own business. I think the house looks fine. It has charm."

"*Charm* is a nice word," she said with a chuckle as she started for the kitchen, but he caught her arm, pulling her back around to face him.

"First things first," Hank said as his arms closed around her and he sought a kiss that she was happy to return.

He felt so good, so big and solid. As if nothing in the world could get through him to her. The kiss deepened, taking on more heat than she expected, and Kit moaned as she pressed against his barrel of a chest.

"You make the sexiest sounds when I kiss you, Kathleen," he said into her neck, his voice rough.

She didn't know what to say to that, and settled for letting him kiss her again, this time taking one of his large, gorgeous hands and settling it over her breast.

"Oh, damn, honey," he muttered, closing his palm over her with more gentleness than she would have expected from such a large, strong man. Kit was learning that everything with Hank was such a nice surprise.

Including his patience. Most guys would have her undressed and against the entry wall by now, but he kept kissing her and moving his thumb over her nipple until she thought she might rip *his* clothes off and push *him* against the wall.

"How hungry are you?" she managed to ask, her breath short as she moved her hands over his broad back.

"Do you have to ask?" he countered with a low chuckle.

She giggled and moved her hand down to slide over him, pleased when he made some nice sounds for her, as well.

"I meant...I was going to cook for you, but, if you wanted to wait for a while—"

It was as far as he let her go, when she felt herself lifted off the floor and swept—for the first time ever in her life—off her feet.

"Hank, what are you doing?"

He held her up in his arms and headed to the stairs at the end of the hall.

"Up?" he asked, desire clear in his expression, his eyes, his voice.

She met his gaze directly. "Yes. Up. Top of the stairs, down the hall, on the left."

He brought her to her room, the one she'd had since she was a girl. She'd never had a man in there, not once. She didn't bring men home, not here.

But Hank was different. As he set her down by the side of her bed and started kissing her again, undressing her as he did so, she knew something with him was very different indeed.

If she wasn't so busy enjoying it, it would have scared the hell out of her. But as he took off his own clothes and joined her on her bed, Kit didn't worry about anything for the rest of the night.

8

ERIN WAS COMPLETELY EXHAUSTED, but from the spot where she sat in the doorway of her sunroom, she could appreciate all of the new changes that surrounded her.

Now, her house was starting to feel like home.

She smiled at her freshly painted ceiling and the summery, soft green walls of her dining room, enjoying how the verdant tone contrasted with the pretty honey color of the room she was in and the rich, cinnamon-brown of the living room.

Hank and Kit were working on the kitchen, which was being redone in sunny yellow and white, and Leroy was retiling her bathroom floor after she had finished painting the room a soft gray with white trim.

Pete was busy on the trim while she'd finished the walls in the entryway—the same honey color as the sunroom—and looked down at her with mock severity.

"No napping on the job, Riley."

"I'm just appreciating the color mixes from a different perspective. I saw it on a design show on TV," she lied, fighting a grin.

All of her blah furniture had been donated, as well.

Someone else might make good use of it, but tomorrow, a new dining and living room set and some decorative pieces would be delivered here.

There were several art shows around the Syracuse area every summer, one in particular downtown in July that was juried, and she couldn't wait to choose colorful, cool stuff to put on her walls and tables. It all made her feel more like herself—or whoever she was becoming. Someone who liked color. Lots of it.

Her smile faded as she thought it would be nice to put up some family photos. Maybe she'd take a photography course and frame some pictures of her own.

The picture of her and Bo on the beach came back to mind, and along with it, a ping of regret that none of those photos could be displayed.

"Hey, no lying down on the job," Leroy said as he came into the room.

Walking up to her, he nudged her with his foot, as if checking to see if she was still alive. She played the game for a second, and then moved fast, grabbing his leg and pulling him down into a wrestling hold that came naturally, though he turned her around and then held her captive in the next second.

"Glad to see you remember some of that jujitsu I showed you, but not enough, lady, not enough," he whispered menacingly in her ear with an evil chuckle. "Loser buys dinner."

She hugged Leroy back, a real hug, not a defensive one this time, and laughed.

"Okay, I planned on treating you all anyway. No need to get violent," she joked as they got up from the floor. "But seriously, you guys do great work. I can't believe how different it looks. And feels. It's a lot more cheerful to be here now."

"It would be even more cheerful with a couple jumbo buckets of fried chicken," Pete said.

"And sides," Leroy added.

"I get it. Food. Okay. I'm going to go upstairs and see how Bo's coming along, and then I'll go."

Bo had joined in when Erin had sent a general invite for a painting party at her place when it became apparent that left to her own devices, she'd never get it all done. With the general invite open to everyone, it didn't make anyone curious about why Bo had joined in.

Dana and Scott had come, and a few other people from the department. It was fun, and the place got done very quickly. She also liked that Bo had chosen to work upstairs. Dana and Scott were with him until they had to leave. Since then, he'd been alone. It had taken all of her willpower to stay downstairs and not go up to see him too often.

Taking the stairs two at a time, she left Pete and Leroy, who were bickering about a sports controversy, and went into her bedroom. The ugly beige was now a soft rose color on one accent wall behind her bed, the others painted in a very pale gray.

"Oh, this is so pretty," she said, making Bo aware of her presence as he put the finishing touches on the trim around her closet. "I can't thank you enough for all of this. It would have taken me forever to do it myself."

She couldn't help but think how he looked at home in her bedroom. He should, she figured, with as much time as he'd spent there in the past two weeks. They'd fallen into a pattern of sorts, much like the one Bo said they had before. They spent evenings and his days off

together, sometimes at his place, sometimes at hers.
In the meantime, she helped with Kit's store and kept
busy.

She had remembered a lot—but it was always from
her relationship with Bo, some family memories, or
events with friends. Like Leroy teaching her some ju
jitsu holds and takedowns. Nothing about the fires or
the job.

At least there hadn't been another arson in that time,
but she couldn't help but wonder if it was only a matter of time.

"No thanks required. This is fun. Relaxing stuff.
How are things going downstairs?"

"We're almost there. Still need to do about half the
trim and finish the bathroom floor. I don't know where
Hank and Kit are on the kitchen. I'll check when I go
back down to get dinner orders, which is why I'm here.
Fried chicken and sides okay with you?"

Bo looked at her and stepped down off the short ladder he was using to reach the upper part of the trim
and crossed to where she stood.

"That's fine, but it isn't really what I'm hungry for."

Then he was kissing her, and Erin didn't mind one
bit. In fact, with the door cracked open, and voices
from the first floor filtering up as everyone worked
and talked, she thought she might have a few minutes
to show Bo how appreciative she was for his help.

Sliding her hand down his chest, her fingers made
their way to the zipper of his jeans and he pulled back.

"Hey, now, we're not alone."

"I know, so you'll have to be really quiet," she said
with a naughty smile.

Bo gave in, bracing one hand against the wall as she

littered kisses over his throat, stroking him in a hard, fast way that she knew he liked.

Someone's voice got louder in the entryway, and they both stilled, but there were no footsteps on the stairs, so she continued. Taking his other hand, she placed it over her breast as she kissed him, and felt him shudder.

His groan was low and deep, and he collapsed against the wall with a resounding *thump* as he climaxed, his breathing harsh, though he made no other sound.

"Hey, everything okay up there?"

Pete must have heard the noise, and Erin smiled as Bo caught his breath.

"Yeah, Bo just dropped a can of paint, but it had the lid on, thank goodness. I'll be back down in a second," she responded.

Bo's chest was still heaving, his eyes hot as he pulled her in for one more kiss.

"You always did like the chance of being caught," he said before he released her, separating so that they could fix themselves up.

She shrugged. "It's fun. The excitement of almost being caught adds a little something."

"Have you ever thought what?"

Erin shook her head. "I don't know. Some adventure, I guess. I do remember the time we had sex under the stands at that concert. That was crazy, with people all over the place, but it was also really, really hot."

Dressed again, he put the lid on the paint can he was finished with.

"That it was," he agreed with a chuckle.

"I guess it's my little bit of kink. You don't have any—or any that I remember?"

Standing, he looked at her speculatively, as if unsure if he wanted to answer. That intrigued her, and she dared him with her smile.

"C'mon, Myers. Confess your naughty secrets to me."

"Nope, not me. I'm kink-free. Straight as an arrow," he said, fighting a smile.

"So you're not going to tell me?"

"There's nothing to tell, Erin."

She took that in, but his tone suggested there was something he wasn't telling her. Why?

"With you, I always thought the sex-in-public thing was maybe because you wanted someone to catch us," he mused, deflecting the topic back to her. "That since we were a secret, it was like tempting fate. Do you think that's what it is now, too?"

"I haven't really given it that much thought, to be honest. It's just a fun thing to do. Does it have to have any deeper meaning?"

"I guess you're right."

What had been a fun bit of sex was suddenly heavy and uncomfortable. Erin didn't want to psychoanalyze her sex life or his, and if she did, she'd see a shrink.

"For what it's worth, if there's anything you want to do that you haven't told me, I'd be willing to try."

She wanted to change the mood between them, and erase the distance that had somehow grown between them.

"That's good to know."

Frustrated and starting to get irritated, she walked to the door, shoving her hands into her pockets.

"Okay, well…I'd better get going before there's a revolt."

She was out the door and down the stairs before he could reply, still annoyed. Whether she wanted to think about it or not, now her mind wouldn't let go of what he'd said.

Was there any merit to Bo's thoughts that she had wanted them to get caught? Why? To make their relationship public or to make it impossible? If they had been caught, would that have pushed them closer or made their breakup even more imminent?

Or was it simply a fun way to have sex that she found particularly exciting?

She headed to the kitchen to grab her purse when another surprise assailed her. Erin couldn't be sure, but as she went into the kitchen, she could have sworn she saw Hank remove his hand from her sister's bottom.

Blinking, she was sure she must be seeing things.

"Erin!" Kit exclaimed, turning pink, though Erin supposed it could have been the exertion of the work she was doing up on the stepladder.

Erin looked at Hank, who was studying the wall he was painting very closely, and she shook her head. Maybe Hank had been steadying Kit on the ladder?

That made more sense. Knowing what she knew about her sister, no way would Kit ever have interest in a firefighter. Though Kit seemed tense lately, too, and worried. Erin had made a few attempts at getting her to talk, but Kit wasn't sharing.

"I'm going for dinner. I'll be back in a bit."

"If you can pick up some cupcakes at Harrison's, that's all I ask," Kit said.

Erin laughed. "I can do that. I love how this is looking," she said, taking in the bright kitchen and white trim. "I'll probably have to have this floor replaced, too. Not right away, though."

"Hardwood is always good," Kit said, and both sisters swung their gazes to Hank as he suddenly was caught by an attack of coughing.

"Sorry, swallowed my soda the wrong way," he said, clearing his throat and turning back to his work.

"Okay, well, I'll return shortly. Thanks for all the help, you guys. This doesn't even look like the same house. Next we'll have to do the outside," she added as she left the kitchen, smiling at their groans of objection.

But as lighthearted as she came off, Bo's comments and her promise to perhaps experiment with him resurfaced as she drove. They were supposed to be reenacting her past, not trying new things, right? But then again, if it was something he really wanted— something she had denied him before—it *was* related to their past. So why wouldn't he tell her? Maybe he was telling the truth, and there wasn't anything. Maybe she was imagining that he wasn't sharing what he really wanted.

Or maybe he'd done that, and she was unreceptive? Or maybe it took a level of trust that they didn't share.

She might never know. Time was getting shorter, and if her memory didn't come back—what then? Bo would be gone, and she would be right where she started, except that now she'd know what a good thing she'd let go.

Bo looked up as Erin appeared in his office door the next day. He wanted to give her a kiss hello, not worry about anyone finding out about them—what did it matter now? He'd accepted the task-force job, and he was out of here in under a month.

But instead, he said hello and gestured to her to sit down.

"Thanks for coming down here."

"Sure. What's going on?"

"I have some news. They're going to start demo on the arson site—yours—tomorrow."

"Oh. Yes, you mentioned that before."

"I wondered if you'd visit the building with me. Take a look before it's gone. I know you went down once before, and nothing came back to you. You also found it upsetting then. Do you think you're okay to go now?"

She took a second to consider. "Yeah, I think it would be fine. I don't know that it will make any difference, but I think I can handle it. I think the time that's passed has helped. When I went, I was just out of the hospital, and I was pretty raw back then."

"If you're up to it, then, maybe we can stop by the second site, too."

"The second fire?"

"Yes. I want to walk you through a few things. See if anything pops for you. There could be commonalities or something you might notice that we didn't. It's a long shot, but it's worth trying."

"I don't know what I could find. I have no connection to that one."

"You never know. You tagged along with me a few times when I was training for arson investigation, as an interested observer. You showed some skill, too—you have a good eye for investigation. But maybe going over there now that you have some distance will make something pop."

"I can definitely try."

"Great. So, we can take the afternoon to do that, and maybe go somewhere after?"

Erin paused, and then met his gaze. "Sure. We could probably stay around here. I mean, I don't think it's a big deal if anyone sees us. No one seemed to think twice about you coming over to help with the house the other day."

"You invited everyone at the department who wanted to help."

Still, his heart—and his hopes—rose at her notion that it didn't matter if people saw them together. He would have given his left arm to hear her say that six months ago.

"I don't think we have to worry. We're out visiting the sites, so that can be our excuse."

Her words brought him back down to earth. "Yeah, but we'll take my truck and come back for your car later. So it's clear that it's just business. Not personal."

He wasn't sure if he caught a slight flinch as he said that, but she agreed and stood, walking ahead of him out of the office.

Things had been tense between them since their discussion at the house, and Bo hoped this went well. It seemed as if Erin's memories were there, but being with him was only triggering relationship memories. And that was triggering all kinds of other complex emotions.

She'd wanted him to share more about his desires at the house, but he couldn't do it. Not when they didn't have a future. What was the point? In truth, he had expressed a few secret fantasies back when they were together, but Erin had been uncomfortable with it because it meant she had to give up control. She had to trust him completely.

And apparently she didn't. Bo had no desire to tread over that territory again. They had to stay clear on the real reason they were doing this and see if they could rouse memories about the fire. That was the goal.

There'd been no activity for weeks, and for that he was grateful, but the investigation had also hit a dead end. Whoever was setting these fires, they were hard to track.

On their way out to the truck, Bo watched her walk. He liked how her bottom moved. It made him think about other things he wanted to do later.

Maybe he shouldn't have mentioned that bit about her maybe wanting them to get caught. He might have been way off. As she said, it wasn't that, but the idea itself was the thrill. That would be more Erin's style, daring the world to cross her.

She'd been good at firefighting because she knew how to stay calm and keep her cool under pressure—the way she did when she was turning him on with all the guys and her sister a few rooms away.

She liked the challenge. She craved excitement. They were alike in that.

Her offer to try something new—anything he wanted—was tempting. It was also dangerous. Did it mean that Erin had changed? That some of the old rules between them no longer applied? That she trusted him more?

That there could be something new between them?

He shook his head as if trying to cast away the thought.

"What?" she asked, bringing him back to the present.

"What?" he echoed back, taken off guard.

She smiled. "You were shaking your head no at something."

"Oh. Just lost in thought, that's all. Here we are," he announced. "If this is bad and you want to leave, you say so, okay? We're only here to look around—no pressure."

"Got it."

They stopped, and she slid out of her seat to the pavement, taking in the skeletal remains of the burned-out warehouse. Erin seemed to confront it without any particular emotion at all. That was a good start, he supposed.

They approached a small shed, where Bo grabbed hard hats and handed her one. She put it in her head, and he stifled a smile. He'd once told her how cute she was in her firefighting helmet, and she hadn't taken it as a compliment. She'd been cranky with him the rest of the day, until he got her back to her place and did things that made her decidedly uncranky.

"Let's go."

He went ahead. No one else was there, though there was heavy equipment on the other side of the lot. They were obviously prepping to level the place. He couldn't blame the company that owned the property—it lost money the longer it sat here unused, and the investigation had held it up for long enough without yielding much. This was Bo's last chance, literally.

The light was fine as the sun came in through the rafters, and safe passage through the burned-out building was marked with small flags and chalk so that inspectors and others weren't injured.

"Make sure you stay within the marked areas. Other spots are not safe."

Erin nodded, but was otherwise quiet. Bo hoped this wasn't a mistake.

"It's so spooky," she finally said when they paused inside the large entry, looking around. "But also weirdly pretty. The way the sun comes down in between the burned rafters."

"I've thought that, too, though it feels wrong to see something artistic in so much ruin."

She agreed silently and walked ahead of him, her expression mostly curious. He let her lead, but made sure she stayed on the safe route. He wondered what it would be like, to see it all again for the first time. Even with his experience, it was still overwhelming sometimes. The ability to analyze discrete parts of a fire scene as well as the overall picture took discipline and practice because there was so much to look at. It was also easy to see something misleading or something that could fool you.

Eventually, you learned the patterns and the telltale signs of various kinds of fire, how it behaved or how it had started or progressed, but there was still an element of surprise. It paid not to get too bogged down in patterns, since that's when you could miss the most important things.

Maybe it was the same way in relationships? What had he missed that he and Erin had gone so terribly wrong?

He pushed romantic musings from his mind. Though he'd been over the site several times now, some things had changed due to weather exposure and other peo-

ple invading the area, and he tried to see it all with
fresh eyes.

What might he have missed?

Erin started moving faster through the charred
walkway, as if she were moving toward something.
As if she were drawn in a certain direction. Bo followed, fascinated.

She stopped at a spot in the far corner, looking up.

"Something happened up there?"

She turned and looked at him, her face strained—
parts fear, anxiety and pressure.

Bo followed her gaze.

"That was the general quadrant of the building that
you and Joe were sent in to check out. They thought
there could be toxic chemicals stored there. But you
were both found in a completely different area of the
building, which is one of the things we can't account
for."

Her expression was pained as she stared, trying to
remember so hard, and Bo almost couldn't take the
agony on her face.

"I can feel something…like, panic," she said, and
he stepped closer as her breathing quickened. "But
nothing else."

He noticed her hand was shaking as she lifted it to
her face.

"This is enough, I think. Let's get out of here."

"No, I'm okay. I'm just so frustrated. Show me the
spot where we fell."

Bo shook his head. "I don't think that's a good idea."

Erin stared through the rafters at the same spot on
the second level for several more long seconds, and

hen, before he could stop her, she took off for the
stairs that went up to that floor. Outside the safety zone.

"Erin!" he shouted, but she was fast and halfway up
he steps by the time he followed.

"I'm okay."

"It's not safe. Those supports are burned. Come
back down slowly."

She looked at him over the rail. "They're knocking
his down tomorrow. I need to see."

She continued her progress up the stairs, which
seemed to be holding, so Bo muttered a curse under
his breath and followed.

Erin was never reckless before, which made her
one of the best. She knew that being reckless was what
could cost people their lives, and Bo hoped that wasn't
the case now.

She was also about sixty-five pounds lighter than
he was, and when he stood on the second step, it gave
an ominous creak.

She'd ambled up fine, but he could take the whole
thing down in seconds, and then she'd be trapped.

Cursing more vehemently, he backed off.

She was up there for a few minutes, quiet, and he
started to worry even more.

"Erin? What's going on?" he shouted up the steps,
wishing he'd never brought her here.

She came to the edge, peered down at him through
jagged, burned-out boards.

"We ran," she said, her complexion as ashen as the
walls around her. Then she looked over his head, back
toward the east side of the building. "Joe took off and
ran that way."

Chills worked down Bo's spine as she pointed in the

direction of the spot where she was nearly killed. He balanced the excitement at her memory with concern for her current safety.

"Okay, good—that's good. Now, come down very slowly, carefully, and show me where."

She looked like a ghost, but she made it back down the rickety steps safely.

Bo grabbed her and hugged her tight to him, relieved, and then held her at arm's length, staring hard into her face.

"Don't *ever* do that again. You could've been hurt or killed. Stay on the damned safety path from here on, or I swear, I'll arrest you and put you in jail for the night."

He wouldn't really—or maybe he would.

He'd replayed the scene of her falling through those stairs about a dozen times while she was up there, and if she couldn't be safe, he was taking her out of here, memory or no memory.

He'd almost lost her once, and he wasn't going to risk it again.

"You're right. Sorry, I know I shouldn't have done that, but I had to get up there. Something made us run. I don't know why, but we took off in this direction."

"Running away from someone?"

She shook her head. "I don't know."

There had been nothing on the second floor that Bo knew of, and it was easy to think you saw something in the room full of smoke and flames. But if she could remember this much, there had to be more there.

Bo slipped his arm around Erin's shoulders as much for support as to make sure she didn't bolt on him again.

"Okay, show me where."

She zeroed in on the exact spot where they had found Joe dead and Erin pinned under a beam.

"What else?" he prompted.

She stared at the spot for a while and then sniffled. When she glanced over at him, fat tears rolled down her cheeks.

Bo was stunned. He had never once seen Erin cry. Ever.

"Nothing. There's nothing else. We came here, but that's all I know. Why can't I remember this? Why can I remember other things but not *this?*"

Sobs took over, shaking her body, and Bo wrapped his arm around her again, walking her out of the warehouse and back into the light and fresh air. Outside, her tears subsided after a few minutes, and he let her lean on him until they did. Another first.

"I'm sorry," she said, sounding miserable.

Bo looked down into her face, wishing he could make every bit of pain he saw there go away.

"You have nothing to be sorry for."

"We don't know that, do we? I remember running and Joe following me, but I don't know why. I led him to his death. It was my fault. Maybe his family is right to blame me."

"No." Bo said the word with absolute conviction. "First, you don't remember enough to know what happened, let alone take responsibility for it. Second, you and Joe were both experienced firefighters. If you knew you had to get out, and he followed, it was a good call, or he wouldn't have gone. What happened next was an accident, or it was someone else's doing. But either way, it is *not your fault*. Don't even go there."

Erin seemed as shocked at his vehemence as he was, but some of her distress cleared.

"Okay. But how can we stop them from demolishing this place? If I can't come back, I may not ever remember the rest."

Bo agreed, but he didn't know if he had enough to reopen the case and stop the demo. A few vague memories wouldn't be much to argue with.

"C'mon. Let's go back to the office and see what we can do to make that happen. It might be too late, but we can try. Then you're going home to relax, dress up in something nice and let me take you out, okay?"

She wiped the tears from her face and frowned. "Okay. Jeez, I hate crying. It makes me feel like such a *girl*."

Bo laughed and hugged her one more time.

"Now there's the Erin I know."

She smiled slightly and Bo smiled back, but it didn't reflect how he felt. Not really. It was good that she was remembering—it seemed like more memories surfaced every day. He couldn't help but wonder how long it would be before she remembered that she hadn't wanted to be with him. Until that happened, he'd be there for her. He'd do his job, and then he'd leave this all behind, as well.

9

ERIN GRIMACED AT the pile of clothes on her bed and made a frustrated growl, looking at the clock. She had four hours before Bo came back to take her for a night out. He'd said to wear something "nice." She wasn't sure what "nice" meant, but she was fairly sure it wasn't anything on her bed. Everything she'd gotten before was casual, flirty, but not necessarily what she needed for a fancier excursion.

She needed to get something appropriate, not that she had much of an idea what that was, and she needed it now. She needed some shoes, too.

Grabbing her bag, she headed for the door. There would definitely be something at the mall, and it couldn't be that hard to find a nice, basic dress and some shoes, right?

Twenty minutes later, she was in one of the larger department stores at the Carousel Center—now also known as Destiny USA. She hoped it was her destiny to find the right dress, and fast.

Spotting the women's department, she approached

a clerk who looked well dressed, and tapped her on the shoulder.

"Yes? May I help you?" The woman was maybe a few years older, but looked like a million bucks.

"Please. I need something nice for a dinner date. A dress, I suppose? Can you find something that would be appropriate?"

The woman stood back and took in Erin from head to toe, making her feel a tad self-conscious, but this was no time to be shy.

"Do you know how nice? Very formal, or less so?"

"I have no idea. He said something nice," she said, rolling her eyes.

The saleswoman laughed. "I think I have a few ideas. Some new styles we just got in from New York."

"Sounds good."

Erin followed the woman, whose name tag said her name was Emily. They arrived at a rack of dresses.

"We'll find something here. I'm Emily, by the way."

"I'm Erin." She stared at the rack, frowning. "They're all black. Don't you think something with more color?"

Emily winked at her. "Trust me. If the key word is 'nice' you can't miss with black. It will fit in anywhere. Especially these, with your figure. You don't need much to be stunning."

Erin couldn't be sure, but she thought this could be the first time a woman ever made her blush. Emily chuckled, grabbing a handful of dresses and beckoning Erin to follow.

"Here, try these on. This one first," she instructed and Erin realized the woman hadn't even asked her size, but she probably didn't need to. The woman seemed to know more about dressing her up than she did, so Erin decided to trust her.

Dutifully shucking her jeans and T-shirt to try on the first dress, her trust was well-placed. The slip of fabric fit like a glove.

"Wow," Erin breathed, looking at herself in the mirror.

It had appeared innocent enough on the hanger, but on her body, there was nothing "nice" about this dress. The soft fabric skimmed just above her upper thigh, and Erin had to resist the urge to tug it down. She could feel air-conditioning from the vent at the side of the dressing room wafting up and cooling her...no, this was too short.

And when she saw the price tag in the mirror, she decided it was also far too much money for so little fabric.

"Erin, do you need any help?"

"No, thanks. I, um, I think that first one isn't quite... me." *Or doesn't cover up enough of me to go out in public,* she thought as she flipped through Emily's other choices.

One designer dress was simpler and offered a bit more coverage, as well as being about a quarter of the price of the other dress.

Erin slipped it on, and she liked how the fabric just fell into place. The V-neck was sexy but tasteful, and the hemline was a more reasonable midthigh. She ran her hands over the folds in the skirt—pleats? They made the plain black fancier.

This one was definitely nice.

Confident, she went out to get a second opinion.

"I like this one?" Erin spoke the statement as more of a question as the clerk eyed her critically.

"Gorgeous! That definitely suits you. The satin crepe really softens and accents your shape. Nice choice."

"Good. Thank you. If you can suggest a pair of shoes to match, you will officially be my hero."

Emily laughed. "Oh, shoes, yes. I know just the pair. And you'll need a bag, and perhaps some stockings? Garters?"

Erin stared. "Do I need all that?"

Emily laughed. "It's good to have at least one entire ensemble. And men love garters. Trust me."

"I guess it can't hurt to try it on."

"I'll be right back."

Erin was sure that the saleswoman was more excited about the shopping than she was, but it was going much more easily than she imagined, so that was a blessing. Sitting down on a bench by the entry to the dressing room, she waited and was glad to find she could sit comfortably—and modestly—in the dress.

"Erin?"

Erin saw Dana standing a few feet away.

"Hey, Dana," she said with a smile, and then saw her friend's curious gaze as she took in the dress.

"Whoa. That's a killer dress."

"Thanks. Emily, ah, the saleswoman, picked it. You know me, I know nothing about clothes."

"You suddenly got the urge to shop? Are you feeling okay?"

They laughed, and Erin shrugged. "I had some time and figured I would pick up a few less-casual things. Just in case, you know?"

"Sure. And you hit the nail on the head the first time. That's perfect on you. I love that designer. I have several of her pieces myself, though now I can't wear them after seeing how amazing they look on you."

"Yeah, right." Erin waved her off. "I'd never heard of her before this." Erin had a feeling she'd never heard of any dress designers.

"Here we go! I have some heels I'm sure you'll like, along with the garters and the stockings. I can show you some evening bags on the way out, and I promise your fella is going to have heart palpitations when he sees you tonight."

"Fella? You're seeing a *fella* tonight?" Dana's stare sharpened on Erin like a hawk's on its prey.

"I have to try these on," Erin said hastily and sought refuge in the dressing room, but not before she heard Dana's warning that she could wait.

Oh, crap.

Leaning against the door for her temporary reprieve, Erin knew the jig was up. Whatever a jig was.

She'd have to tell Dana something, and she was a lousy liar. Especially to her friends.

Focusing on the shoes, she checked out the garters and stockings, but decided to pass, simply pulling on a pair of light gold, strappy sandals that ended up being far more comfortable than they looked.

Taking a deep breath, she headed back out, finding Emily and Dana chatting easily, both turning their attention to her with equal approval.

"Perfect." Emily sighed.

"Those shoes make your legs look a million miles long," Dana said with a low whistle.

Erin was pleased with their reactions, and she had to admit, she felt great, too.

"So what will *your* fella think?" Dana asked, blinking innocently.

"I, um, he…" Erin sputtered and cursed under her breath, retreating to the dressing room and closing the door.

Seconds later, Dana's voice came from the other side of the door.

"Hey, Erin. I'm sorry. I didn't mean to make you bolt. I just… I'm surprised if you have a date and you didn't tell me. Are you okay in there?"

Erin's shoulders sagged. Was she okay?

Hours ago, she was climbing up a burned-out ruin trying to remember one of the most critical events of her life—and now she was standing here like Cinderella getting ready for the ball. Maybe talking to someone about all this could help. Maybe it would make everything stop spinning for a second.

Erin opened the door and stood back, inviting her friend inside.

"I'm sorry. I didn't know I had a date until today, so this is kind of last-minute but…the guy thing isn't. It's actually pretty complicated. I'm starting to feel… dizzy. Like I don't know which end is up."

She sat down on the narrow seat on the wall, deflated.

"Want to talk about it?" Dana joined her.

Erin stood up. "Yes. I have some time before I have to get home and get ready."

"Let's get your things, and we can go walk while you tell me about you and Bo. Iced coffee is on me."

Erin gaped in surprise.

Dana rolled her eyes. "I notice things. Like the look on your face when Bo showed up for painting a few weeks ago. C'mon, change, and we'll talk. I've been dying to know about this for, like forever."

"Erin, is there anything else I can help you with?" Emily spoke from the other side of the door.

"I'm good, thanks, Emily. I'm taking the dress and the shoes. I'll be out in just a second."

"Take your time. I'll meet you at the register."

Erin listened as the clerk's heels tapped on the floor as she walked away.

"How long have you known?"

"I didn't know, but I suspected."

Erin was suddenly nervous. "Do you think anyone else knows?"

"No. You kidding? Everyone else we know is male, and they don't notice that stuff. Get dressed, and I'll meet you out there."

Dana slipped out while Erin changed and gathered up her things, coming to terms with the fact that someone knew—and had known for a while, by the sound of it—about her and Bo. It was…a relief.

They paid for her new dress and shoes and made their way out to the coffee shop, and then walked along the wide aisles of the new mall.

"So you and the marshal," Dana invited. "Tell me."

"Well, like I said, it's kind of…an on-again, off-again thing," she said, for lack of a better way of describing it. "And I don't remember all of it, but that's kind of why we're back together now. For the moment anyway."

"What does that mean?"

Erin wasn't sure how much she should share of Bo's

career plans, as she knew they were waiting until they had a replacement for him before making a general announcement. But after swearing Dana to silence, even with Scott, she told her the whole story—as much as she knew anyway.

"So, let me get this straight. You two were together all last year, you broke up with him, and now he's back with you again, but only so you can remember about the fire?"

"That about sums it up. But he's moving to Virginia soon, so you know...when he goes, that will be that."

Dana leveled a look at her. "And that's okay with you?"

Erin shrugged. "It was the deal."

"That's not what I asked. A woman doesn't dash out to buy special clothes for a guy she's not into—in a big way. I'm worried, Erin. You've been through a lot. Are you falling for Bo, no matter what kind of deal you two had?"

She was about to say no, but stopped. "I don't know. I definitely feel something, I guess. I like him, and we're good together. But without knowing everything, I can't know what's between us. Not really. We broke up for a reason. The idea of him leaving so soon bothers me, but a lot of that is because of what happened today. The building will be wrecked, and I'm remembering some things, but not enough."

"And the fact that he's going means maybe he's not feeling the same things you are?"

Erin shrugged. It pinched to hear the words aloud.

"I can't blame him. I opted out, and this is just... an experiment, I guess. Also, I'm the only one who might be able to help him get more evidence to find this arsonist."

"That's too much pressure for you to put on yourself. It seems to me you have to separate out the fire stuff from the relationship stuff. You're a different person now. Believe me," Dana said with a laugh, looking at her shopping bags. "Maybe what you have with Bo could be different, too."

Erin shook her head. "It's different because I can't remember why I didn't want to stay in the relationship, and he's moving on. He was clear about that. I won't change the rules of the game now. It wouldn't be fair. And you can't tell anyone, Dana, please—even Scott. Okay?"

"I promise. If you promise to talk to me if you need to, when you need someone."

"I will. Thanks. I'd better get going. I still have to shower and get ready."

As they reached the doors that led to the parking garage, Dana put her hand on Erin's arm.

"Erin, please be careful, okay? You've been hurt once, in the fire, but there are a whole lot of different ways you could end up hurt this time. I don't want to see that happen. You've been through enough already."

Erin took a deep breath and smiled brightly. "I'll be okay, Dana. But thanks. I went into this with my eyes wide-open, but it means a lot to know I can talk to you."

After they hugged and parted ways, Dana's parting words lingered. Erin's pace increased across the lot, the anticipation of seeing Bo, and of dressing up for him, giving her an extra zip. Maybe she had changed, and maybe Bo had, too. But she meant what she said.

She wouldn't change the rules of the game now, even if it meant that she was bound to get hurt in the end.

Bo APPROACHED ERIN'S door with a brisk step, hoping he hadn't overdone it as he looked down at the roses in his arms. He hadn't bought roses for a woman in a very long time—the last time was probably for his mother on her birthday. He hadn't ever gotten flowers for Erin, because she never seemed to want that kind of thing.

Maybe she still didn't? He paused on the walk, looking at the roses and his dress shoes, shiny against the concrete, wondering if she might feel pressured, if this was too much.

He wanted to take her away from the ugliness of the fire scene, to take her mind off it completely. But she'd never been much for dress-up.

Well, he had reservations, but he could cancel them if need be. Whatever she wanted, he could go with the flow. That's what he told himself as he continued to the door and rang the bell.

When the door opened, he almost dropped the roses.

"Incredible," he whispered, taking her in as she stood before him, nervously raising her hand to her hair to push it back, and then frowning, as she often did, still forgetting it was short now.

Without saying a word, she invited him in, and Bo accepted, unable to take his eyes off her.

The black dress hugged her curves and fluttered down over her hips in soft folds that made her ultra-feminine, her long, bare legs exposed, the pretty gold sandals she wore making her look like some fairy-tale creature. His gaze drifted up, lingering on the way the deep neckline exposed the swell of her breasts and made his mouth go dry. Her short hair combined with the V-neck made her throat impossibly long and graceful. He swallowed, wanting to taste her there, his cock twitching with interest inside the loose dress pants he wore.

"You are insanely beautiful, do you know that?" he said roughly once he was inside the door, setting the roses down on a nearby table. He needed to touch her to make sure she was real.

"Thank you, I—"

It was as far as he let her go before he kissed her, hands on her shoulders, their bodies not quite touching, but he breathed her in as he touched his tongue to hers.

"You smell like…gardenia."

Nothing strong or overwhelming, but he could pick the scent up on her skin as he came close.

"It's a new soap I bought."

"It's perfect. Like you."

She smiled, her cheeks turning pink in a feminine manner that made him even harder.

If he didn't reroute his thinking, they'd never get out the door. Taking a step back, he picked the roses up again.

"These are for you," he said, presenting them to her.

Her lips parted with pleasure as she brought them to her nose.

"They smell wonderful, thank you. That's the signature of a good flower, you know, the scent."

"Don't they all have scent?"

Bo was again captivated by how the dress swished around her bottom as she crossed the room in front of him.

"Not a lot of the ones you find in grocery stores,

and that kind of thing. I forget why, Kit told me. Some are made that way to not aggravate allergies, but others are just made to be…well, generic, I guess."

"Interesting."

Though, really, all he wanted to do was watch her move in that dress, go to dinner, and then get her alone and take it off her.

"Thank you. They are gorgeous," she said admiringly, putting them in a vase on her new dining room table.

"You're welcome. The place looks great, by the way—you've added new pieces."

She smiled widely then, genuinely pleased as she looked around at her new, renovated surroundings.

"I love it. It feels more personal now, like a home should."

A home—something Erin never seemed to care about much before. Bo cleared his throat.

"We have reservations in a half hour. Are you ready to go?"

"I am," she said brightly, picking up a small black bag with a gold chain. Bo didn't even know she owned clothes like these. She looked elegant and sexy in every possible way as she walked out to the door.

He was glad he'd brought his car instead of the truck.

"Oh, my, that's yours?"

Erin stood by the side of the classic black sports car, looking like every man's fantasy. Bo wanted to put her on the hood and push that dress up—

"Bo?"

He snapped out of his thoughts with a chagrined smile. "Sorry. Yes, that's mine. It was my father's. We worked on it together for years, and he left it to me when he passed on. It's a '67. My pride and joy. I only take it out of the garage for the occasional summer drive and a special occasion."

"It's beautiful," she said admiringly, running her hand over the edge of the roof.

Bo joined her, opening the passenger-side door. "I'm glad you like it."

And he was. Erin had admired the car before, and they had taken a few drives in it, but tonight felt different. He'd wondered if she'd remember. They'd driven the GTO to the apple orchard on their last real date, but apparently none of that was coming back to her as she buckled herself into the luxurious ivory leather seat.

He got in and did the same, heading to the highway, loving the growl of the engine as he did so.

"Where are we going?"

"The inn, in Skaneateles. Do you remember it?"

"Not really. I know the town, but don't have any specific memories of the restaurant. Did we go there often?"

"We went to the pub a few times, but not all dressed up like this."

"Speaking of which, you look great, by the way. I wasn't sure what to wear. I was so relieved when I saw you were dressed up, too."

Bo grinned. "Sorry about that. I wondered the same, on the way to the door, if I had overdone it."

"I'd say we did just fine."

"Agreed."

They drove through the winding roads of the countryside between Syracuse and the small Finger Lakes town to the southwest of the city, enjoying the view. Bo drove slowly along the main street by the lake, enjoying the attention the car always drew, but this time, it was eclipsed by the attention Erin drew after he parked and helped her out.

There wasn't a head that didn't turn as she strolled down the street, and he tucked her arm into his possessively, letting people know she was absolutely taken.

And then he caught himself, realizing he'd forgotten again that this wasn't what it seemed to be.

Erin seemed to pick up on his tension, and put her other hand on his arm, facing him.

"Bo? Everything okay?"

He smiled, leaning in to kiss her cheek. "Yes, sorry. I forgot if I'd locked the car," he lied smoothly.

She relaxed again, too, as they progressed up the stone steps in the inn and were shown to their table.

It was a reminder that this was a fantasy, but he saw no reason not to completely enjoy it anyway. He ordered some wine and watched Erin as she studied the menu, not wanting to look away, as if she might disappear. As if he was imagining it all.

But when she smiled at him over the top of the card, her eyes bright, he knew it was 100 percent real. As were the very dangerous emotions clutching at his chest.

Their waitress arrived and took their orders, and Bo put the worrisome thoughts away for the evening. Right now, he was here with the most beautiful woman he could imagine, and he wanted to embrace it. Live in the moment, that's what they always said, right?

This arrangement with Erin was what it was, but that didn't stop him from having feelings for her—which was why he'd done all of this in the first place.

Because he cared. He'd never stopped caring. It didn't change anything.

"I think I remember walking down by the lake...out on the pier? Something funny happened? We laughed really hard?"

"Yes, that was one day last summer. There was a guy proposing to his girl out there. He wanted to make a big deal, and managed to crawl up on the rail, proposing from there for everyone to hear. When she said yes, he got so excited that he lost his balance and fell in the lake. He was fine, and had to swim the few yards to shore. He was yelling how much he loved her all the way in," Bo said with a grin, remembering, too.

"Yes," she said, staring out the nearby window at the water. "I think I remember some of that. A young man."

"Very. Who was also fined by the local police as soon as he hit the shoreline, but he didn't really care."

They laughed, and it lightened the mood. Their wine arrived, and an appetizer, then their entrées. Bo loosened up as they chatted about this and that, nothing having to do with the fire or anything serious.

But then Erin asked, "So, the new job? Do you have any more news?"

"It's official. I'm heading down the second week of August, and they should have a new investigator ready to take my place here in a week or two. He's experienced, so it won't take long to bring him up to speed. We got lucky in that way. I'll need to go down a week ahead to get an apartment, that kind of thing."

"You're excited," she said with a smile.

"I am. It's what I've been working for all these years. It will be challenging, but I can't wait, really."

Her smile faded, and he wanted to kick himself.

"I mean—"

She reached over, covering his hand with hers. "No, I completely get it. And you should be excited. I'm excited for you. This is incredible."

"Thanks," he said, letting it drop and turning his hand so that he could rub his thumb over the inside of her palm.

The touch made her eyes darken, the mood shifting quickly between them.

"It might have been presumptuous of me, but I reserved a room upstairs for the night. But we could go home, if you want to," he said.

Erin wrapped her fingers around his, squeezing. "A room here is a nice idea."

Bo's heart picked up speed as he paid the check and took her hand, pulling her to his side.

"I couldn't agree more."

10

ERIN EXPLORED THE beautiful room, decorated with antique furniture including a huge, comfortable bed that looked out over the lake. She took the chance to enjoy the view as Bo retrieved their dessert and wine order from the server who brought it to their door.

"I knew you were ordering some wine, but champagne? You're really going all out tonight, Myers," she said with a smile.

Their eyes met, and she took a breath. "That's the first time I've called you by your last name. Like I used to do."

He looked down at the tray, grabbing the bottle of wine, and Erin couldn't tell if he was happy about that memory or not. She also found it disconcerting when old behaviors suddenly appeared, like a name or some bit of knowledge slipping from her lips unbidden.

The pop of the cork made her jump, and when Bo looked up again, he was smiling.

"Grab a glass," he said easily. Erin smiled back, glad he was okay. She was reading too much into everything.

She held both glasses while he filled them and then took one after he put the bottle back in the holder.

"To old memories," he said, raising his glass.

And to making new ones, she wanted to add. Instead, she softly echoed his words instead, and clinked her glass to his.

Bo pulled something from his pocket, setting it on the dresser. Music started to play.

The song... Erin felt it before she could remember anything. It was important. Emotion swamped her, and she felt tears come to her eyes, but she couldn't remember.

"Tell me about that song, Bo. I know it's important, but I don't know why."

"We went to the concert at the fair last year. The band kept doing encores, and we kept trying to leave, as did a bunch of other people. We all made it to the parking lot, but then they started playing this song, and all the people in the lot started dancing. So we did, too. It was the only time we'd ever danced."

"It sounds like magic."

"It was...special."

"There's more. I can see it in your face. What happened?"

Bo took a deep breath. "When we were dancing, told you I loved you."

Erin felt a flutter in her chest. "Oh."

"And you didn't say it back."

"Oh," she repeated, crossing the room to stand i front of him. "I'm so sorry."

"No need to apologize. It was too soon for you. didn't mind telling you, and sure, it would have bee nice to hear that you felt the same way, but it didn't change how I felt."

"I wish I could remember."

So she hadn't loved him? Even she couldn't believe that, given all of what she did remember and what she felt now. Not that she wanted to think about that, but it was what it was. She couldn't deny it.

Bo's hand cupped her jaw, then fell. "Me, too."

He put his glass down, and Erin stepped in closer, taking his hands in hers. "I don't know what was going on in my head then, or what my reasons were. I don't know why I was...like I was. But if I said I didn't love you...I think I was lying. I don't know why, but I know it's true."

"You don't need to say that."

"I'm not just saying it to make you feel better. I'm saying it because of how I feel now. I know I loved you...I can still feel it. Right here, right now. I still—"

She stopped, aware of what she was about to say, and unsure if she should. It wasn't fair to either of them, was it, to say such things?

"Erin." His voice was so soft she wasn't sure if he'd spoken at first, but when she looked up into his eyes, they were so raw with emotion, so hungry, that she felt it down in her soul. "Say it."

"I don't think—"

"Please."

Erin didn't know what had stopped her from telling him before, but it seemed like the most natural thing in the world now, the words leaving her lips with no effort at all.

"I think I did love you then, Bo, but I know I love you now."

He gathered her in, crushing her against him in his arms, as if she were life itself.

"Erin, I never stopped loving you. Even when it was killing me, I still wanted the pain. And now, to hear you say it…I know this thing we have isn't about love but—"

She pulled back, staring up into his face. "But it can be tonight. I know you have to go, and I don't know what I'm doing next, but we have right now. Tonight."

"Yes," he agreed. "It definitely can be for tonight."

Erin didn't remember anything from her past as Bo kissed her as though he cherished every taste, every touch, but she suddenly didn't care so much about the past. The present was all that mattered.

She loved Bo. She could feel it in her bones, in her blood. Whether she could remember or not, if she had denied it in the past, then she'd been a liar.

The realization made her want to show him how she really felt. Maybe she wanted, to some degree, to make up for how she had hurt him before. She hated that she'd caused him such pain, and placed both hands on either side of his face, showing him the same tenderness he was showing her.

Breaking the kiss, both of their pulses had picked up. The song playing on the iPod he'd left on the dresser ended, and she smiled into his face.

"I think maybe we need a new song."

Leaving him for a second, she went to the device and flipped through the playlist, finally finding one that she loved.

As Nat King Cole's melodic voice, joining his daughter in a duet, and the strains of "Unforgettable" filled the room. Bo laughed softly as she went into his arms.

"Perfect," he said.

They started to sway, dancing in the small space by the window, and Erin knew peace for the first time in months.

But that changed to something hotter as they moved together, and Bo's lips whispered over the skin of her throat, moving up to her lips, and then back down, lower, tracing the vee of her dress. Though he didn't touch her there, her nipples hardened at the proximal contact, and she let out a soft sigh as her head dropped back.

His hands found their way down over her hips, bracing her bare thighs on either side, his skin hot. Pressing his mouth to the inside of her knee, he slid his hands upward, moving her skirt upward, as well.

"I've been dying to know what you're wearing under this dress," he said.

Suddenly, Erin wished she'd bought the garters and stockings, but then took that back as Bo's thumbs grazed a very sensitive spot through the thin silk of the panties she wore, making her gasp. The other accessories would have only been barriers to his touch, and Erin wanted nothing between them.

"Very nice," he said, taking his time as he looked at her in the black bikinis she'd bought on the way out of the store, made of silk and lace, with a tiny bow on the front. Like a gift, which was exactly how Bo treated them.

He pulled them off gently, letting her step out of them without catching them on her shoes, and then worked his way back up her leg in a path of hot kisses that ended right where she needed him.

"Yes, Bo, please," she begged as he widened her stance, the skirt of her beautiful dress crunched in his hands as he knelt before her, and flicked his tongue out to taste her.

He murmured huskily against her sex, using nothing but his mouth to send her into a breathless frenzy of need.

She murmured his name as she felt the tension winding too tight. He looked up curiously, concerned, and she smiled.

"Together" was all she needed to say.

He stood, and she led him over to the bed, taking her time as she undid his tie, then the buttons on his shirt, pushing it off with his jacket. Leaning in, she brushed her lips over the rough hair on his chest, over one nipple, then the other, liking the male groan that followed.

Turning around, she waited for him to unzip her, and let the dress fall to the floor around her feet. He unsnapped the bra as well, and she shrugged that off, turning back to him.

The way he gazed at her, naked before him, made her feel like never wearing clothes ever again.

Wordlessly, she divested him of the rest of his clothing until they were both completely naked to each other. Her hands trembled slightly as she embraced him, pressing herself against him, his hardness eager against her hip.

The kiss went on forever, as she wanted it to, and when her blood heated even more, she pulled away and lay back on the bed.

"You're too far away," she said, holding out her hand to him.

"I love looking at you."

"There are far better things to do with me than look," she said with a smile that made him smile, too.

In the next second, he was there, next to her, over her, pressing her down into the mattress as the kisses deepened and the need swelled.

They both went as slowly as possible, making every touch last, every kiss linger, until Erin couldn't take it anymore. Wanting to be completely connected to him, she parted her thighs, urging him down in between.

He slipped inside her, slow and easy, planting himself deep as he watched her face, never taking his eyes from her.

"I do love you, Bo. Whatever happens after this, right now I need you to know that."

"Oh, Erin, I love you, too. Always will," he said, coming down for one more kiss as he started to move.

Erin was feeling too much as he pushed her higher, her body wanting everything that his had to give, but also feeling, inevitably, like this was a hello and a goodbye at the same time. It made it all unbearably emotional as the pleasure gripped her, making her shudder under and around him, their arms wrapped around each other so tightly she was surprised they could move at all.

Bo took his time, rocking into her in a steady rhythm as she whispered delicious, naughty words to him. Telling him what she liked best made him lose control in a way that ended in a bone-racking orgasm for both of them, leaving them spent and exhausted, and still twined together as they drifted off to sleep. Erin wasn't anxious to see morning come at all.

KIT PLUCKED PINK-WHITE peony petals from her hair as she let Hank pull her up to standing and straightened her dress. She looked at him with a tender smile. He also had flower parts stuck to him, including one large pink petal that she peeled from his cheek.

Sex in her backyard garden. Amazing. The sex, and the man.

Luckily, Erin had felt guilty for disappearing the day before—and all night, as well—and had come into the shop early, offering to stay for as long as Kit needed her. Her sister didn't say where she'd been, and Kit decided not to ask her. It wouldn't do any good anyway. Still, Erin seemed different—tired, but happy. And smelling like gardenias, which was interesting.

Kit had decided to take the opportunity to come home for lunch only to find Hank weeding and pruning, applying fertilizer like a pro. Of course she did tell him none of it was necessary before she'd seduced him, right there in the yard. They had fences, and the neighbors were at work anyway.

Her knees still had grass stains, and looking down, she was pretty proud of that fact and that she'd ridden Hank into submission right there near the peony patch.

"You surprise me," he said, leaning down to kiss her again, stirring the embers that hadn't quite settled yet.

"You surprised me, too. I didn't expect to find you out here in the garden."

"I know you have your hands full, and I had some extra time. I forgot how much I missed this. I used to have a small garden, but the more the department demands took over, the more I let it go. I think I'll try to get it going again."

"That's a great idea."

They went inside where it was cooler, and Kit washed up at the kitchen sink.

"I took up most of your lunchtime," Hank said, watching her. "Why don't you let me buy you lunch before you head back to work?"

She loved the way he looked at her, how he focused on her. She'd never felt so much the center of someone's attention before, and it was very nice. But it was also a problem.

It made some of the problems in the rest of her life go away, at least for the time that they were naked and sweaty together. Like the fact that she'd hardly seen Erin for most of the week, and that she was nervously waiting on a loan that could give her shop a second chance and save her from taking drastic action to solve her financial worries.

Like selling her mother's home and getting an apartment.

If she had to, she would—it would probably be easier to maintain, and the money would help her keep the business going.

But it broke her heart to think of leaving this house.

"Hey, you okay? Why so sad all of a sudden?"

She'd become completely lost in her thoughts, and forgot Hank was watching. He was too perceptive. She enjoyed his close attention when he was making love to her, but not so much when he tried to read her.

"Nothing, really, I just need to get back. I'll bring a yogurt from the fridge and I'll be fine. Thanks, though."

Kit was shutting him out, she knew it. She had to. She enjoyed Hank's company, and the sex—well, the sex was outstanding. But he was getting too close. She'd enjoyed finding him here when she came home, but he was always doing something for her. Helping at the shop, bringing her food, weeding her garden… making her lose her mind in bed.

But she knew it wouldn't last. Just like the garden she loved but had ignored, this fling, or whatever it was, was doomed to eventually suffer at the demands of his work. He'd been on his off-time rotation, and then had a few vacation days he'd needed to take—as soon as he was back on the job, she would fall to the background. She accepted that and didn't want to make it any harder than it had to be.

"Kit, what's going on?"

"What do you mean?" she asked as she pulled some yogurt and a banana from the fridge, stuffing them in her purse.

"You're hot, and then you're cold. I don't know if I did something wrong. Did I step in something here?"

She took a deep breath, not having the time or the energy for this right now.

"No, you're fine—wonderful, in fact. I would much rather do what we did out in the garden than eat, believe me," she said with a naughty smile in his direction.

Make it about the sex and keep it that way, she told herself.

"Yeah, that was good, but there's more to it, isn't there? You look like you have the weight of the world on your shoulders."

"It's nothing. I really appreciate your help, but I can't

talk about this right now. I have to get back to the shop to meet a bridal party in thirty minutes."

"Sure, whatever you say," he said, turning his back and grabbing his jacket from the chair. It had some grass stains on it as well, where he'd been on his back in her yard, with her lying on top of him.

She'd hurt his feelings. Cursing under her breath, she closed the fridge and faced him.

"Hank," she said, catching him as he was at the door. "It's just… I have a lot going on. That's all."

He nodded slowly. "Sure, Kath. I get it. I wish I could help."

"That's kind of the thing. I appreciate your help, I really do—but I need to handle things on my own. It's just who I am. I appreciate all that you do, but—"

"You'd rather I didn't do it?"

His cool expression and the flat look in his eyes clutched at her chest. She liked Hank, she really did, but it was all too much. Still…

"Yes, kind of. It's hard to explain. I guess that I don't want to be dependent on anyone."

"There's a big difference between letting someone help and being dependent on them," he said reasonably.

"It feels the same to me."

"You don't always have to do things alone, you know."

Kit wasn't convinced. How did she tell him about all the years she watched her mother do exactly that? Handle everything in the house, the finances, her two children, alone? Because her father was at the station most of the time. And after that, how Kit had started her business, cared for her mother, alone, when Erin had been too busy with the job?

Kit was used to relying on herself, and it was safer that way, she finally realized. When you only depended on yourself, no one else could let you down.

"It's how I've lived for so long, I don't know any other way," she said, helpless to explain it to him.

"Maybe it's time you learned. I know you're afraid. And I know why."

She was surprised, and he met her eyes knowingly.

"I know what you must have gone through, with your dad, with Erin... I can't promise that the job won't take me away from you sometimes, but when I can be here, I will. Completely. I want to be here with you, more than just about anything. Do you believe me?"

She wanted him to leave, and she wanted him to stay. It was like being two people: one who needed to focus on her business and protect her heart, and the other who wanted more with this beautiful, generous man. One who yearned for what he could give her. One who wanted to run away from it full tilt.

But both sides believed him.

"I want that, too, though it scares the heck out of me."

The words were out before she could stop them, the part of her that needed him winning. His expression cleared, his eyes warming, and her world felt right again. She couldn't stand to see him hurt, especially when she was the one doing it. She didn't want him to leave and not come back. Fear grabbed at her heart at the same time hope lifted it.

She was a mess. That was so, so bad, but she couldn't deny it.

He leaned in for a gentle kiss. "It's going to be okay, Kathleen. You have to have some faith."

She let him pull her into a hug, unsure exactly what he meant. Faith in what? But she was tired of thinking and enjoyed his strength for a few more minutes before pulling away.

"I actually do have to get back. See you tonight, around seven?"

"I'll be here. Promise."

She took a deep breath, feeling better about the day knowing that Hank would be there at the end of it. She might be foolish, but she couldn't help herself. He was becoming necessary in her life. It was frightening, and it was wonderful.

Only time would tell which side of that contradiction would bear out.

11

BO SAT AT his desk, buried in files, making notes that hopefully would make some of his caseload easier for the new guy coming in. They were supposed to meet this morning for an initial discussion about the change-over. They would announce his exit and introduce the new marshal at the end of the week.

It was really happening. In another two weeks, he'd leave Syracuse forever. Leave Erin forever.

It had been four days since he and Erin had spent the night at the inn, and he'd been buried in reports and new information coming in from the FBI. They were getting him up to speed on their new cases as well, so he could hit the ground running when he got there.

"Sir, the court made them delay demolition on the site, but only until the end of the week," Bo's assistant informed him, poking his head around the corner.

"Thanks, Rob."

Three days? That's all he had to try to see if Erin could remember anything more? And a week after that. Then they were done.

The guys around the station knew, of course, that

he was leaving, short of the official announcement, and they were taking him out that evening for a few beers. Strangely, Bo didn't feel like celebrating. He was excited about the new job, but he wasn't excited about leaving.

Not since the inn. Not since Erin confessed her feelings to him and stirred that awful hope that maybe something was still viable between them. She'd changed. She was more open, more willing to share. More loving.

He'd loved her before, even when she was distant, but that distance was dissolving. Still, he wasn't going to pass up this job on the chance that he and Erin might reconcile. He couldn't trust anything they felt or shared right now, since she wasn't herself—not the Erin he'd known. He was a port in a storm, perhaps—of course she'd feel something for him, but whether it was a permanent situation was highly questionable. He couldn't base his future on it.

The heavy workload he'd be taking on with the task force would be a welcome distraction.

To that end, he'd checked into one more possibility to access some of Erin's more-buried memories: a hypnotist. He'd gotten a good recommendation for a guy named Stuart Fox from Dr. Higgins, and had called him that morning. Fox was happy to help if Erin was okay with it. Given her qualms about losing control in any situation, he didn't know if she would be.

Another knock on his door interrupted his thoughts, and he looked up to see Erin smiling at him.

"Hey, you weren't due here for another hour," he said with a smile, standing. He wanted very much to kiss her hello, but couldn't. Not here.

She shrugged. "I was over at the hospital for a checkup and driving home. Decided to stop by early and see what you wanted to talk about."

Erin's hand came forward, touched his lightly, sending heat flashing through him. He stepped back behind the safety of his desk.

"Is everything okay? With your checkup, I mean?" he asked.

"Oh, yes, fine. No problems. They were impressed with my progress, actually."

"That's good news. I have some, too. We got a slight delay on the demo of the warehouse site, so we can go back to see if it jogs any more of your memories, but we only have until the end of the week. Come Monday, it's gone."

Her relaxed expression became tense. "Only a few days? I mean, it's worth trying, but I don't know if I'll remember any more than I did last time."

"I know. Anyway, I had an idea. This is completely up to you—if you say no, it's no, but I spoke about the case with a hypnotist. I thought that if he could come with us to the site, put you under, maybe he could help you remember more. He comes very highly recommended."

She frowned as though she'd eaten something sour. "A hypnotist? You believe in that stuff?"

He had to smile at her sharp skepticism. Sometimes, Erin's old self peeked through the cracks of her new self, and he enjoyed being with both.

"I don't know, but from what I've read it's worked in a lot of cases, helping witnesses remember more details and events. This guy is also a clinical psychologist who specializes in regression therapy. In other words, taking people back to their pasts to see if they can solve current problems. He's worked with the police quite frequently. I don't think he's like the hypnotists who run magic shows and would make you cluck like a chicken," he added with a smile.

She was quiet, and for a few heartbeats Bo thought she might decline. Then she shrugged, though she didn't seem entirely happy about the notion.

"Sure, why not? As long as he doesn't do the chicken trick."

Bo grinned. "Maybe only if I make a personal request."

She stuck her tongue out at him, and he enjoyed the playful exchange.

She eyed the large stack of files on his desk. "I guess I should leave you to your work."

Her tone suggested a reluctance to do that, and her eyes were warm in a way that told him she wanted him.

Here? Now?

The idea got him hot, made his pulse beat faster. Rob was across the hall, but Bo's door shut. He could tell Rob not to disturb him, could close the shades, take her over his desk...

"Yes." She said the word as if reading his mind.

Bo didn't have much time left with her, and he wanted them to indulge every minute they could. Walking to the door, he cleared his throat, calling Rob.

"Yes, sir?"

"Could you run this package over to the courthouse for me? I know it's lunchtime—feel free to take some extra time, if you want. I'll hold down the fort."

His younger counterpart didn't seem to pick up on

any unusual vibe, his eyes lighting up at the prospect of an extended lunch hour.

"Sure, no problem. See you in an hour or so."

Bo nodded and waited until Rob had cleared the hall before he closed his door, facing Erin. Her color was high, her eyes excited.

"Now no one will interrupt."

"Good."

He pulled the shades tightly closed, and then she was on him, her arms around him, her mouth on his as if she were as desperate as he was. He didn't waste time, taking her shirt off and pushing his face into her breasts, inhaling her soft scent as he pushed them close together, taking both nipples in his mouth at once, making her moan loudly.

He was ready, almost frantic, and worked the button on her jeans.

"Damn, you make me so hard it hurts," he muttered, slipping his hand down to stroke her, finding her as ready as he was.

As if she knew what he wanted, she turned around, braced herself on the desk, looking back at him with clear invitation.

There was little finesse for either of them, only scorching need.

"This is why I came early. I had to have you… didn't want to wait," she managed, and then groaned softly as he traced his lips along her spine.

Bo could only show her how much he appreciated that decision as he held her hips in his hands, finding a quick rhythm that pleased them both as their sighs and moans mingled in a shared climax that nearly made him black out for a minute. He wasn't even sure if he'd shouted her name or if anyone could have heard, and he didn't really care.

Still breathless, he pulled her back against him, wrapping his arms around her. "It seems to get better every time, doesn't it?"

"Yes. Very much so."

Her head dropped back against his shoulder. He found her mouth, kissing her tenderly until the heat started building between them again.

It had to be the time frame that was responsible for the urgency he felt. The driving need to have as much of her as he could. She quivered against him as his hands closed over her breasts, kneading gently. He didn't tire of her, wanted her constantly. Looking into her face, he saw the reflection of his own desire. She felt the same as he did.

It had always been good between them, but not like this. Not so…intimate. So *shared*.

"I love you." He couldn't help saying it.

She smiled, and his heart lit up. "I love you, too."

A car door slamming outside his window brought reality back, and he let his hands drop from the warmth of her body. They both took a minute to quickly straighten their clothes.

"Ladies' room?" she asked in a hushed voice, the door outside creaking as whoever was in the lot came into the building.

"Down the hall, to the left."

Footsteps went past his door. They both let out a sigh of relief and laughed.

"Let me know when you want me at the site with the hypnotist," she said on her way out.

"I will. Where are you going now?"

"To help Kit for the afternoon. I've been flaking out on her lately, so I might take her out after she closes the shop."

Bo felt a ping of regret that he wouldn't be able to see her that evening, but offered a smile.

"It's nice that you two are closer. Tell her I said hello."

Was there a flicker of something like disappointment in her eyes, too?

"I will. Um, bye."

As she started to leave, he called out her name.

"Hmm?"

Bo held her gaze, not wanting to let her go. At least, not with this sudden awkwardness that had settled between them.

"Thanks for coming by, Erin, especially coming by early," he said with a wink, enjoying how it made her blush even more deeply. "If you want, give me a call when you get home tonight. Or come by. I'll be up."

Pleasure suffused her expression, and Bo felt immediately better, having reasserted the connection between them.

"I'll talk to you later, then," she said, and then she was gone.

Bo sat down in his chair, dropping his head into his hands. He wasn't making this any easier on himself, but he had a feeling there was no way to do that anyway. He'd let himself fall for her again—as if he'd ever stopped being crazy for her. Not that it mattered. He was leaving, and she hadn't asked him to stay.

He blinked, staring at the wall. Had he really thought she might? Would he if she did?

ERIN DIDN'T IMMEDIATELY get out of her car once she'd arrived at the warehouse as planned. Bo's truck was here, and a silver-gray sedan alongside it. They were waiting for her.

Bo had offered to pick her up, but after the encounter in his office the day before, she'd needed some space. She hadn't been lying—she did go work at the store for the rest of the day, and offered to take Kit out. Or to stay in and watch TV, having some sister time.

An offer that was politely refused as her sister had other plans.

Kit didn't tell Erin what those other plans were, but Erin suspected a man was in the picture, if her sister's sexy new haircut was any indication. Kit had been quieter than usual, but she seemed happier, too.

When Erin tried to tease an answer out of her, Kit had maintained that she was only meeting a friend and had proceeded to hide in the back of the shop with a new shipment of summer flowers.

Erin had felt…slighted. Kit was obviously keeping a secret, and didn't want to talk to her about what was going on in her life. Erin supposed turnabout was fair play—she hadn't told her sister about anything going on in her life, either.

Had it always been this way? She wanted to be closer to Kit, but they felt further apart than ever.

When she'd gotten home, she also hadn't called Bo, even though she'd said she would. He hadn't called her, either.

The sex in his office the day before had been hot—wildly so. If not for the location and possible interruptions, she was sure they would have kept going. It had been difficult not to call as she sat home alone that evening, thinking about him and wanting him fiercely. She'd tried to read, watch TV, but all she could think of was Bo.

Not good. Not when he would be leaving by the end of the next week.

They'd gotten closer. Admitted feelings for each other. That they still cared. It was more than sex, but he was leaving nonetheless. He hadn't asked her for anything more.

Taking a deep breath, she got out of the car and headed toward the entry that they'd used the last time, finding Bo and another man just inside the door. Bo had an extra hard hat in his hand and passed it to her.

"Hi, Erin, thanks for agreeing to try this," he said, sounding very businesslike. He flipped his gaze to the man standing across from him. "This is Dr. Fox, the man I told you about."

Erin studied the man who smiled at her. She didn't know what she was expecting, but the doctor lived up to his name.

Total fox, absolutely. He wasn't tall—not as tall as Bo, and not as built. More like a runner, thin, but still nicely put together. In his late thirties, he had an angular face that accented intense dark gray eyes. A shock of dark blond hair kept falling forward over those eyes, making him absolutely rakish.

"Nice to meet you, Dr. Fox," she said.

"Nice to meet you, too, Erin. I've read up on your case—quite interesting. I've never had a client with complete amnesia before, or at least, as complete as yours has been. I can only imagine how difficult the past months have been."

His voice was unerringly masculine and sympathetic without being overly so. He had a kind face and a nice smile. His hands were slightly roughened, which made her wonder what he did to earn the calluses. She decided that she liked him and relaxed.

"So, Doctor, how does this work?" she asked, smiling brightly at the two men.

Bo, however, wasn't smiling. He looked...strange. Tense.

"If you'd please show me what happened the last time, and where—as much as you know—we can begin. Then, I'll try to put you into a light trance and take you back to the day of the fire to see if we can tease any more details out of that brain of yours," Dr. Foxy—er, Dr. Fox—said with another thousand-watt smile.

"Sounds good."

"This time, stay on the safety path," Bo cautioned her sternly. It was all he said before they went in.

Surprised by his abruptness, Erin fell into step with the handsome doctor, who didn't seem to notice if there was any tension between her and Bo.

"So, have you ever been put under before?" he asked.

She shook her head. "Never. They mentioned it once, early on, in the hospital, but I couldn't do it then. I was just too freaked out."

"Completely understandable. Most people think having a clean slate, erasing their pasts, would be great—but the past is what makes us who we are. And how we react to it, grow from it, or not. Some people don't have amnesia, but they push events from their pasts so far down into their minds that those things sit there like a thorn, festering. It can be very damaging."

"That's what Bo, um, Marshal Myers, said you specialize in? Getting people to remember their pasts?"

"That is my particular interest, yes. Though hypnotism is a mainstay of my practice, I address a range of mental health issues with my clients. But dealing with past life trauma has been my main interest since college."

"Past life? You mean, like, in reincarnation?" she asked.

"No, I haven't gotten into that, particularly—that's more of a spiritual venue. But certainly childhood events that are forgotten, or milder cases like yours, where a trauma has gotten in the way of a memory surfacing."

Erin noted that they were approaching the spot where she had climbed up on the rafters a few days before. Looking at them now, she realized why Bo had been upset—what had she been thinking?

She hadn't. She'd only been feeling.

"So what do I do?" she asked as they stopped. Bo faced them, still quiet.

"Tell me what you do remember."

Erin did, as best she could. He listened, nodding every now and then as she spoke.

"It's good that you have a tight link between your emotional responses and the memories that are surfacing. Those emotional cues are very important—what would you say is the dominant emotion you remember as you and Joe ran through the building?"

His gray eyes homed in on her as though he could see through her—disconcerting—but Erin reached back to remember.

"Fear."

"Anything else?"

She shook her head. "Maybe...I don't know. Something like urgency, or worry...anxiety, I guess."

"Understandable, given the situation. Okay, so I'm going to put you into a gentle hypnotic trance. You may not feel like anything has happened. You'll feel awake, but very calm. You'll be able to hear us, and be aware of everything that goes on around you—maybe even more so than normal. You are not losing control or being controlled, and no one can make you do anything you don't want to do. We'll be here the whole time, and you will be perfectly safe."

"So how will I know if it's successful?"

Fox's gray eyes sparkled, and he winked. Were doctors supposed to wink?

"Believe me, we'll know."

"Okay then, let's do it."

Erin slid a glance in Bo's direction and felt more reassured when he held her gaze, his own confident and sure.

"It's better if you can sit, so that you don't lose your balance or fall. On the floor is fine, if you're okay with that."

"Sure." Erin dropped into a cross-legged position and looked up.

"Find a spot, something in the building to concentrate on—a small spot of light, or a shadow...whatever your eyes can latch onto, and don't look away...."

Erin did so, finding a glimmer of sun through some broken boards. Dr. Fox continued his patter, and she felt herself relax. She felt calmed as she listened to him, appreciating his voice even more as her eyes drifted shut. He started counting back, back through hours and days. The little sliver of light she'd been staring at began to move, and before she knew it, it wasn't light, but a flame dancing in front of her.

"There's a fire. We have to get out," she said, panicked, worried about Bo and the doctor. How had this place caught on fire again? She started to push up from sitting as the flames got bigger, smoke overcoming the space.

"We're fine, Erin. You're safe, and so are we. That fire is one you are remembering. It's only a memory and is no danger to us right now, okay?"

She had to catch her breath, slowing her heartbeat as he spoke. He was right. She could see the smoke and the flame, there wasn't any heat, no difficulty breathing.

"Okay. This is weird."

She heard the doctor chuckle again.

"You have a sexy laugh," she said, feeling like she shouldn't have said that, but then again, why not?

"Thank you. Now that you know you're safe, let's go through what happened when you came into the building with Joe. Can you walk us through what happened?"

"Joe's dead," she said, tightening up again.

"Yes, he is. But there's no danger to you now, okay? Do you believe me?"

"Yes."

"Fine, so tell us what you see."

Erin tried, peering through the smoke, looking for Joe.

"We were supposed to check the second floor in the back corner and make sure there were no chemicals. Joe went up the steps first. They were fine—the fire hadn't done much damage on this end of the building yet."

"That's great, Erin. You're doing well. What then?"

She saw Joe, in her memory, disappear at the top of the steps, and she walked up behind him.

"There's so much smoke. I can't see."

"Take your time. See if you can clear the smoke. Find Joe. What's he doing?"

Erin tried, but she couldn't see past the smoke, and her heart started to beat fast again, her entire body tensing.

"I can't see him."

"Okay, it's okay. Calm down, take a breath. Think about something happy, a color you love, or a place or person that makes you happy."

Erin's mind went directly to Bo and how she felt when she was close to him. The only time she truly felt safe.

"Okay, that's good. Now, let's skip ahead to you and Joe running from the spot—do you remember what you saw that made you run?"

The smoke thickened again. She could remember running, Joe behind her—she needed to get out. But everything was dense, gray and white, impenetrable.

"I can't find him. I can't see anything," she said loudly. The harder she looked, the less she saw.

"Bring her out of it, now," she heard a voice say, but her mind was lost in the smoke, looking for Joe.

"Erin, listen, I want you to think about a different place, a place that makes you happy. You aren't in the warehouse anymore, and there is no fire." The doctor waited a beat. "Are you there?"

She focused hard, and then apples and blue skies

opened up through the smoke. She was snug in Bo's arms on the ground. Her tense muscles relaxed into his warmth.

"Yes. Yes," she repeated, her breathing coming more easily.

"Good. You did great. I'm going to count back from ten. When I get to one, you'll wake up easily, feeling completely rested. You will remember everything that you saw in your memories, okay?"

"Okay."

The doctor counted down, and Erin opened her eyes, her gaze still fixed on the sliver of light at the end of the building.

Dropping her head into her hands, she said, "That was...disconcerting."

"You were terrific," Dr. Fox said, beaming a smile at her.

"I didn't remember anything." She didn't feel so terrific about that.

"You did, actually. You remembered being at the fire and you will remember more each time, if you want to continue. It's a gradual process, like peeling layers from an onion. Obviously what happened is very difficult for you to pull forward. We might need to talk about that more, those underlying feelings of fear and anxiety, to see if we can get past them to what happened, but you are definitely off to a good start."

Erin tried to be encouraged, but she only felt as though she had failed again. They needed this information *now*.

She pushed up from her spot on the floor and met Bo's eyes. She expected him to be disappointed, let down, but his expression only showed his concern.

"Bo, I—"

"It's all right, Erin. You did your best. Maybe if you can keep working with the doctor, like he said—"

Just then, Bo's beeper and his cell phone went off at once.

He answered and from the look on his face, she could tell it wasn't good news.

"What happened?"

"There was another fire, and some of our guys were hurt. They're being taken to the trauma unit now. Have to go."

He was running toward his truck before she could say another word. Offering a quick goodbye and thanks to the doctor, Erin took off after him.

12

Bo ARRIVED AT the E.R. first, and Erin was right behind him, watching three ambulances pull up and deliver firefighters from their doors. All being raced into the building. It didn't look good.

Her heart was slamming against her chest as she met Leroy and Bo at the entrance. Leroy looked wrecked.

"Leroy, what happened?" Bo asked the firefighter, who was pale even under the grime and soot that covered him.

"Hank, Joanne and a member from one of the volunteer stations were working on the back of the building. It wasn't even that bad. Someone started shouting, and we saw a kid hanging out of a window on the second floor. Hank went in to get him, Joanne went after him. But the guys in the cherry picker got there first, pulled the kid out. The chief radioed Hank and Jo to get out, and then it was like the place just exploded around them."

Leroy's voice choked, and he looked away.

Bo planted a hand on his shoulder.

"C'mon. Let's see what's happening and then I'll go to the site. They're still working the blaze?"

Leroy nodded. "I should be there, but the chief told me to go with Hank, you know, so he wasn't alone, in case... Well, he doesn't look good. Took the worst of it, they said. Joanne and the other guy, Kyle, I think, were conscious when they took them out, but Hank wasn't."

Bo turned his head away for a second, and Erin frowned. Hank was a friend. He was a man that she and Bo had both stood shoulder-to-shoulder with in fires. She couldn't remember it exactly, but she knew it was true. He'd come to the hospital for her almost every day.

He was a good man.

Not *was*. Not yet.

Her chest tightened with fear, her eyes swelling with tears that she choked back. This wasn't about her. She needed to be there for them. Still, she couldn't help but wonder if this had all happened because she couldn't remember enough to stop the person who was doing it.

"Was it the same as the others?" she made herself ask, her voice rubbing across her throat like sandpaper.

Bo shook his head, looking grim. "No way to know for sure yet, but I will find out, and if it is I'm going to track this bastard down if it's the last thing I do. I won't be leaving until I stop this."

Erin stepped back. She agreed and she understood—but part of her cringed. Bo would stay for his job, but not for her.

Again, not important. She needed to focus now on her friends.

"What can I do to help?"

Bo would probably tell her to go home—she was

a civilian. But no doubt he saw the worry in her eyes, her worry and her guilt. Leroy left them for a minute to speak to a nurse, and she welcomed the time alone with Bo.

"Are you okay?" she asked gently.

"No, I won't be okay until this is settled," he snapped, and then shook his head. "I'm sorry. I hate to say it, but this has rattled me."

"It's normal. It's right that it should. I wish I could have helped stop this."

"It wouldn't have mattered, not today. There's nothing we could have done about this," he said.

"I know. Doesn't make it any easier. I need to help, somehow."

"There's nothing you can do, officially," Bo said. "I need to collect as much information as I can here and then get to the fire. I—I may not be around much. Just so you know."

Her heart took a hit, but she nodded as if it didn't matter.

"I know. You have to do this. I get it."

Erin found herself longing to reach out, to touch him, to comfort. But that wasn't possible.

"Joanne's husband will be here soon. I'm not sure about the other firefighter, the volunteer, if his family has gotten notification. You and Leroy should look into that, be here for them," Bo said, his tone masking any emotion, all business now.

"I can do that. You go, don't worry about us," she added, meeting Bo's gaze.

He gave her a short nod and he left. Heading to the nurse's station, he didn't look back, and somehow, Erin knew that this was it. This was the end of what they'd had together.

Leroy came back over to her.

"Joanne and the other injured man, a volunteer, were both conscious and are being treated for some serious but not life-threatening injuries.

"Hank, though, has been taken directly into surgery," he said, chilling Erin's spine.

"He'll pull through. Hank's a bull, he's tough, and he's going to be okay."

She wasn't sure who she was trying to convince.

"You're right," Leroy agreed, pulling her into a hug.

She hugged him back and then saw, over his shoulder, some more of the crew, dirty and still in their gear, crowding in the door, along with police and some distraught people, probably family members.

They broke apart and went to meet the crowd, sharing what they knew, and civilian or not, Erin felt included. Needed.

She thought back to how the trauma nurses and counselors had helped her in the first days of her waking up. How these kind, patient strangers had kept her sane. She echoed some of the things they told her as she comforted Hank's sister, Lily, and helped her make the call to his parents. She listened as some of the crew talked out what happened at the fire, and what they'd seen. Erin held Pete, who couldn't hold back tears.

After several hours, Hank was finally out of surgery, stable but critical, someone finally said. Erin spared a glance at the clock.

"Oh, no, it's so late. Kit is going to be so worried. I completely forgot to call her," she told Leroy, excusing herself.

Dialing the house, no one answered, so she tried Kit's cell. Finally, her sister answered.

"Kit, where are you? I thought you'd be home by now."

"I decided to come back to the store to get some work done."

Her sister sounded strange. Choked up and nasal, like she had a cold.

"Are you okay? You sound odd."

"Yeah, I'm fine. Where are you?"

Erin hesitated. "I'm at Upstate. There was another bad fire today, and several of the guys were hurt, one badly. Hank Aaron? I don't know if you—"

"What did you say?" Kit's voice came out on a hush of disbelief.

"Um, there was a fire. I wasn't there, but a lot of the guys were, and it was bad. I've been here all day, trying to help, and waiting for Hank to get out of surgery, and I lost track of—"

The line went dead.

"Kit?"

Erin looked at her phone, and couldn't believe her sister would hang up on her—even Kit wasn't that resentful—she must have lost the signal, or had a dead battery. Well, at least she knew where Erin was, which was all she wanted to contact her about anyway.

She went back to the group, watching from a distance as Hank's sister talked with a doctor and listened intently, nodding every few seconds.

That was encouraging, Erin thought, hopeful.

"Hey, I didn't think I'd see you here again so soon," someone said from behind her, and Erin saw Tom, on of the trauma counselors who had helped her through her ordeal.

"Hi, Tom. There was a fire, and friends are involved, so here I am. Just trying to help."

"How are things going?" he asked.

"Okay. Good, I guess. I'm remembering some things, and trying to get back to normal."

"Good to hear. I have to get going, but don't be a stranger."

Tom moved on down the hall as Hank's sister turned away from the doctors and rejoined the group. She stood next to Erin, who took her hand and squeezed it as Lily fought through tears.

"He's stable. He has serious head injuries from the explosion, and some internal bleeding, but they think he'll be okay. The next twenty-four hours will tell," she said, choking on the words.

Erin took Lily into a hug, letting her cry it out.

"I'm sorry. It's just so hard… We're so proud of him, and everything he does, but it's always in the back of your head, knowing this can happen. And when it does, it's not like knowing about it makes it any easier."

"It could never be easy. You're doing great. Hank would be proud of you," Erin said easily, but under her comforting exterior, she was realizing exactly how hard it had been on Kit when Erin had been the one coming out of surgery.

And how hard it had been on Kit and her mom when her dad went off to work every night.

It had been hard on Erin, too, but she fought her nightmares about what could happen to her dad a different way—she ran into them. She studied fires—

lived them, even as a kid—and followed her dad where he went rather than staying back.

It hadn't stopped her from losing him, but it made her feel closer to him. But further from everyone else. Something she hadn't quite understood until right now. It was so hard for families, being on the outside, but hurting just as much. Maybe worse.

Talking to Lily in quieting tones, Erin was suddenly surprised by the sound of Kit's voice in the hall, calling her name. Then her sister was there, grabbing her arm, looking frantic—and frightened.

Erin felt sick as she hugged her sister. "Oh, Kit, I'm so sorry—did you think I was hurt? I was trying to tell you, but then the phone cut out—"

"Hank? How is Hank, Erin? Please, tell me."

Erin was blank for a second, caught off guard. "Hank? You mean our Hank? From the crew?"

Kit nodded, swallowing hard. She'd obviously been crying all the way over to the hospital.

"Yes, Hank Aaron. We—we've been seeing each other...."

Erin was blindsided again, and unsure she'd heard right.

"You and Hank? But... For how long?"

"Are you Kathy?" Lily cut in, overhearing them, as they were standing right by her.

"Yes, that's me."

Kathy?

"Hank has told us so much about you. He's over the moon about you, you know. We've never seen him like this with anyone," Lily said, smiling through tears.

Kit was crying now, too, and Erin watched them, trying to catch up.

"I'm crazy about him, too. But is he... How is he?" Kit asked, her voice thinning with fear.

Lily reached out this time, pulled Kit into a hug. "He'll be okay, I think. It's touch and go right now, but I think he'll be okay. Especially knowing he has you waiting for him."

Erin listened, wanting badly to ask about a million questions, but unsure where to start. Her sister had been seeing Hank romantically all this time? And neither one of them had said anything to her?

"I know this is a surprise," Kit said, turning back to Erin. "For me, too."

Her sister involved with a firefighter? It was like someone suddenly saying the sky was orange instead of blue.

"How long?"

"Just over a month."

Erin's eyebrows flew up, and then she closed her gaping mouth and took a deep breath. That was about as long as she'd been with Bo—and it wasn't as if she'd shared that with Kit, either. As sisters, they were pretty much failures, or at least, Erin was. She had so much ground to make up.

"Well, you couldn't have chosen better," Erin said as she hugged her sister again. "If you're going to date a fireman, you might as well accept that you're part of the crew now, too."

Kit wiped her teary eyes and seemed more pleased at that idea than Erin would have imagined as they joined the guys and listened to their conversation. Lily appeared again, touching Erin's elbow.

"They said I could see Hank for a minute. I asked if you and Kathy could as well, and they said yes, but just for a minute or two each. He's sedated, and he looks pretty bad, they warned, but he'll know we're there. They said it might do him good to hear our voices."

"Absolutely," Kit said.

"Why don't you and Kit go first, and if he's up to it, I'll go in then," Erin said, garnering thankful looks from both women.

Her sister was clearly head over heels—one more huge reason Hank had to make it. She was going to be sure to tell him so and paced the hall outside the ICU, waiting for her turn to visit him.

After what seemed like a longer time than it was, Kit and Lily emerged from the ICU, both teary but smiling, looking better. Erin rushed up to them.

"How is he? How are you?"

"He's sleeping, like the doctor said, and hooked up to so many machines, but when Kathy—Kit—touched his hand and spoke to him, his heart rate spiked," Lily said with a smile.

"He knew I was there. I think his fingers moved a little, next to mine. He was really trying," Kit said, starting to cry again.

Erin hugged her sister, repeating how sorry she was that Kit had to go through this—again. Her sister had been through enough—too much. Erin had never realized it before because she'd channeled her emotions differently—or buried them altogether. Thinking back to how she was with Bo, how much she had held back from him, how distant she'd kept herself…regret swamped her and tears flooded her eyes, too, until all three women were weeping and then laughing about it.

"What a sight we make," Kit said, reaching into her purse for a tissue.

"Let me go say good-night to Hank, and I can drive you guys home, if you need me to," Erin said.

"We'll wait here."

Erin entered the ICU, stopping to wash her hands with the antiseptic and covering her mouth with the mask they provided to visitors before she went into Hank's room.

He looked awful, and she had to swallow her reaction before she stepped in closer. He was bruised and cut everywhere. Machines beeped all around him, and Erin found herself standing by his bed, shaking uncontrollably, unable to speak. She was overcome with emotion.

Had she ever told Hank how great she thought he was? Or had she only engaged in the playful banter that they all did, their way of managing the fear and the danger? It was something to keep sane, but when you managed your whole life that way, it didn't work out so well.

At the bottom of that defense mechanism was fear—ugly, snaking fear that threatened to rise up any moment and drag you back down. You could deny it all you wanted, but it was still there. The problem was that you could only avoid it for so long. Sooner or later, it had to be faced.

Erin was facing it right now, more so than she ever had in the past. She'd never really been afraid while entering buildings or dealing with danger, but this—being helpless, being hurt, seeing her friends or family hurt—this scared her.

"Hey, Hank, it's Erin," she said, sounding froggy. "So, you've been dating my sister, huh? We're going to have to have a talk about that when you wake up.

She's special, and she's been through enough. You're a great guy, the best guy I could imagine for her—so don't hurt her any more, okay? You make sure you get through this, because she needs you. So…just get better fast. Okay? I'll be back to see you tomorrow. Promise."

Erin gasped softly as she thought she felt Hank's fingers move slightly under hers, though she couldn't be sure if she imagined it. She hoped not.

Turning to leave the room, Erin paused, feeling dizzy, so she grabbed Hank's bed rail tightly enough that her fingers hurt. Light-headed as she closed her eyes, she could hear the beeps of the machines, the murmur of the ICU staff working just past the curtain. Then she was brought back to her own bed, when she'd been injured, yet now she stood there, listening…remembering it all.

She was at the warehouse. She could see the smoke, and the flames. And Joe.

The smoke eventually cleared, and visions stuttered behind her eyes as if they were playing on an old projector that was missing every other frame, but she saw enough to understand.

And then she remembered some more…and sobs began to shudder through her body as in one stark, painful flash, she knew everything again.

Bo HAD BEEN working since the night before at the hospital, spending hours at the site, and then at the labs and with the police. This time, their arsonist had messed up—this time, setting explosions, he'd left evidence behind. He'd gotten sloppy, thinking the structure would be vaporized, and the evidence with it.

Not so much.

It was a common error among stupid criminals. They thought they could use fire to hide a murder, for instance, but not anymore. It took a very hot fire and a lot of time for a body to completely incinerate, and with modern methodologies, they could detect all kinds of trace evidence on what was left.

Bo had managed to speed up the processing of the evidence, using his new FBI connections to pull in a favor—it was a bit presumptuous as he wasn't even part of the team yet, but the bureau was more than happy to help. And it had the resources to do it ten times faster.

So for now, Bo had slept at the station, waiting for a call with some news. A name or a place—someone they could close in on.

He didn't want to be in his office. He'd worked in this station for a lot of years. It still felt like home, especially tonight. Truth was, if he was ruthlessly honest with himself, he didn't want to go back to his place without Erin. He was feeling the personal stress of recent events and what had happened the day before— who wouldn't?—but being at his apartment alone was impossible right now.

He wasn't sure what he could do about that. Maybe in Virginia, in a new place, it would be easier. *Yeah, right,* the little devil in his head mocked him.

The guys were out on a call, back to work even after the tragedy of the day before. But someone was moving around down in the kitchen, so he decided to go and see who was there, feeling restless.

Turning the corner, he was surprised when he saw Erin. Bo started to walk into the room, but something made him hold back, watching her from the hidden corner. She seemed to be looking for something, grabbing a chair and climbing up on it, running her hands over the tops of the kitchen cabinets.

He hadn't spoken to her since the hospital, though he heard that Hank had woken up and was off the critical list. He had a long recovery ahead of him, but the signs were promising.

She reached the vent above the cabinets and pulled at the grate—Bo was surprised when it gave way easily, not screwed in completely. How did she know that, and what was she after?

Erin reached into the vent, grabbing something, and then scrambled down, putting the chair back and pulling her phone out of her pocket. She had something in her fingers—an SD card?—and jammed it into her phone, and in the next few seconds, another voice filled the room.

"You don't know what you're missing, girl," a man's voice taunted.

"Leave me alone, Joe, I mean it. This has to stop. I'll report you if you keep harassing me like this."

"Yeah, you think anyone's going to believe you? Especially when you've been screwing Myers for months? Why not share the wealth? No one has to know—it can be our little secret."

Bo's mind reeled as he listened to Joe's voice on the recording playing from Erin's phone. He could see her hands shaking as she held it, even from where he stood ten feet away.

The recording went on, and he could make out the sounds of a slight physical struggle—Joe had touched her. The man had put hands on Erin—not in a good way. He'd known about her and Bo, and he was using that to try to get Erin to sleep with him.

Anger like Bo hadn't known before shot through him, and his hands fisted at his sides. So that was what she'd been keeping from him. He'd been able to sense it back then, especially when she was increasingly cagey. He'd asked, but she never would tell him.

Judging by the tape, she hadn't told anyone. Handling it herself, as always.

Some of his anger and hurt extended to her—why hadn't she come to him? Why had she taken on this guy alone?

And how had she known the recording was there? Had she known all this time? Or had she just remembered? Had she been holding back? It was time to find out.

Finishing off the recording, Bo was relieved to know Erin had come out on top of the struggle. Joe backed off, but Bo knew that probably hadn't been the end of it. Guys like him were predators—they didn't stop until they got what they wanted.

Bo composed himself as well as possible and walked into the kitchen, as if he hadn't been there all along.

"Oh, Erin," he said in false surprise. "What are you doing here?"

She looked up quickly, guiltily, and shoved the phone into her jacket. All of the color had drained from her face, her eyes wide and dark. She swallowed hard, and he wanted to grab her, hold her and let her know no one else would ever hurt her like that again.

But she regrouped quickly, though she didn't meet his gaze. Putting her mask in place.

"Bo. What are you doing here? I didn't think anyone was around. I heard the call come in on my car's radio."

So this was a covert op, he mused. She'd been waiting for the place to empty out.

"I worked late. Didn't want to stay at the office. So I came over here to bunk down and see if there was anything I could do to help. The crew was pretty unsettled by the explosion yesterday."

She looked down at her feet, at the wall, out the window. Anywhere but at him.

Bo had planned on confronting her, but now, he needed to see what she did. Put the ball in her court. What play would she make?

"I came by to grab some things of Hank's—apparently he was seeing my sister all this time, well, for the past month. I had no idea."

Bo was surprised, too, though he was more interested in the fact that Erin clearly wasn't going to tell him what had happened to her and why she was here. She was obviously upset, agitated, but covering it up. Why would she cover for Joe now? Why not tell him? Why lie?

"Kit said Hank had some things here in his locker that he asked her to get, but she had to stay at the store—so I offered to come down. Of course, I forgot the key to his locker," she said, furthering the lie.

Or maybe it was partly true, who knew? Who cared? Her act hollowed Bo out and made what they had together more of a sham than it already had been.

Suddenly, he just wanted her gone.

He also didn't want her to leave.

He wanted to shout at her and make her tell him why she'd kept everything from him, and why she wasn't confiding in him even now. She'd said she loved him, but how was that possible when she couldn't trust him? Be open with him?

"I can let you in, I have a master."

She blinked, her bluff called. "Oh, okay, sure."

Bo was numb as he took out his key and watched her rifle through some of Hank's things, pulling most of them out before closing the locker.

"Great, um, thanks."

"Sure."

They stood there in awkward silence, until she asked, "Any news on who did this?"

"We should have a name soon, I think. We're closing in on a possible suspect. I'm waiting on a call."

No sooner had he said the words than his phone rang.

"Sorry, I have to take this."

"Oh, sure, please. I'll...talk to you later."

He didn't respond as he took the call. The news was good. They were sending in a squad to the suspect's last known address, and Bo was going to be there. The FBI would have a presence as well, since the guy in question was a suspect in several fires spanning multiple states. He had more than one burned building and dead body behind him.

Bo started to tell Erin, but when he turned around, she was gone.

So that was it. They were over. It was just as well, he thought, grabbing his gear and heading out.

13

In the hospital lobby, Erin signed in and got her visitor's badge before taking the elevator up to see Hank. He was awake and talking, and had even called her from his room asking if she could make a lunch run before her visit—he hated the hospital food.

She'd been glad to do it, and the prospect of seeing her old friend—one she could now remember clearly—bolstered her day. And she'd needed the boost.

Bumping into Bo the previous afternoon had been unexpected—and she'd panicked. She hadn't expected anyone to be at the station, which is why she'd offered to go get Hank's things. She remembered hiding the recording in the kitchen, but she didn't know exactly where it was. She needed some time to nose around for it undetected.

She'd almost been detected in a big way. But Bo was distracted by the investigation, which worked in her favor. Everyone had been talking all day about the arrest they made the evening before. The arsonist was a man who'd been tossed out of the volunteer department he'd once joined for drinking on the job, and never let back in. He obviously harbored a dangerous grudge about that.

So he'd been taking it out on innocents and other firefighters in the two years since. His fires had been widespread and unconnected as he moved from place to place, leaving sadness and ruin behind him before he moved on.

But as it ended up, he hadn't set the fire that had hurt Erin and Joe. That had been an arson, but their suspect had been seen fifty miles away that evening. Now the investigation was focusing on the company that owned the building and its employees.

Erin's injuries and Joe's death had nothing to do with the serial arsons. It only made her decision about what *she* should do about what she knew all the more confusing. Now it seemed even less relevant to expose what had happened—Joe was gone, and his family would be the ones to suffer if she revealed what she knew.

Then again, his family deserved answers, and Erin deserved to be cleared of any suspicion in what happened. His family still could bring a civil case against her or the department, though they hadn't. Yet.

She walked into the hospital room and stopped short, seeing her sister draped over Hank like one of his blankets, the two obviously sharing a moment.

"Oh, my eyes! My eyes, they burn," Erin cried dramatically, grinning and turning her head away.

Kit looked up, her hair mussed, her eyes all blurry. Hank still looked bruised and battered, but he was smiling now, somewhat blurry himself. Not from drugs though, Erin thought.

"You could have simply knocked," her sister said drily.

"Eh, what's the fun in that? I can leave if you two aren't done making out."

Hank had recovered sufficiently to be moved from ICU into a regular room—a private one—so they had room to sit and visit. But as Hank and Erin discussed the particularities of the case, Kit became increasingly quiet, eventually excusing herself and leaving the room.

Erin watched after her and sighed.

"Maybe you should go talk to her, since I can't," Hank suggested.

"Let her have some space. We're alike in that—we don't like to be pushed or crowded."

Hank grinned. "Yeah, I noticed that."

"I'll go check on her in a few minutes if she doesn't come back. She's always had a hard time with the job. I can't blame her."

Hank watched Erin closely.

"Why do you think that is?"

"I didn't really understand it myself until you were hurt, and watching what Lily went through, as well as Kit. Me, too. When we were on the crew, we couldn't afford to feel too much of it, in case it got in the way. I think I had to be outside of the job to really get it."

"Get what?"

"That the only way to do the job is to shut everything inside off. To shut off the worry and the guilt. And the fear. But that causes its own problems."

Hank looked at her shrewdly. "So you remember more about the job now?"

Erin bit her lip, and shifted closer to Hank. "I think I

remember almost everything. When I was in here with you, when you were out, that first night… I don't know why, but everything started flooding back."

Hank's eyes went wide. "Seriously? And you've kept this to yourself because…?"

Erin released a long breath. "It's complicated. There's been so much going on, and some other things I need to take care of."

"Like your relationship with Myers?"

Erin sat back in her chair. It was her turn to be surprised.

"What do you mean?"

"What, you think we're all as dumb as we are pretty?" he said, making her laugh. "No one could miss the chemistry with you two, and it's been back in spades. It's obvious when you guys are anywhere within a mile of each other."

"I see. I guess I was the one in the dark, then. I had no idea everyone knew."

"Not everyone, but a few of us who noticed. And I saw you out with him more than once, clearly not wanting to be seen. Why the secrecy?"

Erin frowned. "Back then, I didn't want anyone to know. I thought you would all think less of me, or think I couldn't do the job. You know how it can be for women sometimes."

Hank nodded. "Other places, sure. But you were among friends. None of us would have thought that."

Some did, she thought darkly of Joe. It was one more reason not to tell anyone about what happened— it would be a stain on their station's otherwise honorable reputation.

"I guess. But this time, it wasn't a reconciliation so

much as...a temporary thing, and a conflict with him investigating the case. So we had to be careful. And anyway, there was no point in letting everyone know when it was temporary. And now over, by the way."

"Why does it have to be over? Do you love him?"

Erin thought carefully before answering. "We have too much history. And he's moving on."

"Whose excuse is that, yours or his? Have you even talked about it? Does he know your memory is back?"

"No. You're the only one who knows right now."

She hadn't told Bo because she hadn't been able to face him again until she could figure out what to do about Joe. Or maybe she never wanted him to know. What would he think?

"Erin, if you don't mind me saying so, you and your sister are pretty messed up."

She laughed in shock. "Oh, really?"

"Yes. I love you both, but you need to start relying on and trusting in others—especially the people who love you—including each other. Including me and Bo. Starting there, perhaps. Maybe if you trust in Bo, trust that it can work out, it will. In spite of her fears and what happened, Kathy's put her trust in me. In us. She's not bailing. You shouldn't, either."

"It always sounds so weird to me when you call her that," she said lightly, but only because she needed to be light in response to his words.

"Go talk to your sister, and then go talk to Bo. If nothing else, clear the air before he leaves. You both deserve that."

Erin let her head drop back, closing her eyes as she digested the truth of Hank's words.

"You're going to be such a pain in the ass to have in the family, with all your wisdom and stuff," she said.

"You'll get used to it."

Erin stood, giving him a gentle hug and a kiss before she took off to find her sister. She found her, standing by the window near the end of the hall, staring out.

"Hey. Sorry if the shop talk got out of hand in there. Are you okay?"

Kit gave her a faint smile. "I guess it's something I have to get used to. He's worth it."

"He is. You, too."

"I had doubts, you know. Every day since I've been with him, I'd think, 'I should end this before it goes too far,' or, 'I must be crazy getting involved with this man,' but I just couldn't not see him. He has my whole heart. And last night, when you called, I thought I lost everything, and that he'd never know how much he means to me."

Tears fell freely down her sister's face, and Erin had to choke back her own.

"I think we both learned to avoid pain and fear, to shut it out, growing up. It was how Mom dealt with things—but not how we have to."

"You didn't avoid anything. You don't fear anything," Kit said.

Erin coughed in disbelief. "Are you joking? I think I've been afraid every day of my life. I also worried about Dad, and I grieved when we lost him—but I handled it in a different manner. I needed to be close to him, so I followed in his footsteps. And in doing that, I wasn't as close as I should have been to you because I saw loss all the time, but I couldn't face my own. I didn't want to ever lose anything again."

Kit looked at her in stunned amazement.

"I know," Erin said, shaking her head. "It took literally losing everything to learn this. But…it's all back. Or I think most of it is. The other night, in the room with Hank…I just started remembering. Everything."

Kit flung herself at Erin then, wrapping her in a tight hug, murmuring thanks over and over.

"I'm so glad. So, so glad."

"Thanks," Erin said, feeling connected to her sister for the first time in a long time. "There's something else. I was seeing a man back then, and the reason I wasn't around much lately is because we started up again, but it's been kind of a mess…."

Erin told her sister about Bo, as succinctly as such a tale could be told, and Kit listened, not interrupting until she was done. She also told her about Joe. It was time she confided in someone, certainly in her sister.

"Oh, Erin, what a terrible thing you were living with," Kit said, leading her over to a bench where they could both sit. "I guess we've both been dealing with a lot—and not too well—when we could have been sharing the load."

"Well, I don't know that I would call Hank a load, exactly," Erin said with a grin. "Although he is a big man."

They laughed, but Kit was serious again. "No. It's more than that—Hank has been my joy for the past few weeks or so, but the store… I think I'm going to have to close. Business just isn't great, and unless I mortgage the house or sell it to keep going, I don't think I can stay above water. And I don't want to sell that house or go into debt. I'd kind of like to raise my own kids there, if that ever happens."

And the surprises kept coming. Erin had no idea her sister was dealing with such problems and felt terrible for being so out of touch.

"I'm so sorry, Kit. Is it that bad? There's no other solution?"

"Not that I can think of. I'm competing with all of the places that people can get their flowers less expensively. I could change my inventory, but then I feel like I'm selling out. What I sell makes me different from all the other guys—maybe too different."

"Hank was right. You and I are a mess," Erin said with an unhappy laugh.

"At least we have good men in our corners."

"You do. I mean, Bo is a good man, but we're over. We were over a long time ago. This was just…a mirage."

Kit made a raspberry sound, sticking out her tongue. "Give me a break."

Erin blinked. "Um, way to go with the sisterly sympathy."

Kit shook her head. "There's sisterly sympathy— and believe me, my heart goes out to you about what happened with Joe. I wish he was alive so he could be flayed for what he did to you. But then there's tough love. You and Bo…you're obviously meant for each other. You light up just saying his name. You can work it out, if you both want to. If you don't want to, then maybe it's better this way."

"You didn't hear the part about him leaving? Taking on a new job? I saw him yesterday, when I went to the station to get Hank's things—he was cool. Detached. He hasn't called. Believe me, I know *over* when I see it. The message was loud and clear."

"And you're just going to let it end like that? Again? You said he always sensed you were holding something back, that you didn't trust him, not completely—and that's still the case, isn't it?"

Erin frowned. "No, I do trust him, but—"

"There is no but. Either you do or you don't. All-in or not, Erin. If you trust him, and if you love him, you need to tell him everything and see what happens. That's what trust is. That's when you know you'll have really faced your fears. Believe me, I know. I faced my worst one in the past few days. All I knew was that I wanted Hank to live and to be in my life—regardless of his work. Which reminds me—are you going to be a firefighter now that your memory is back?"

Erin shifted, surprised at the question. Funny, she hadn't even considered that since her memory returned. Weeks before, the job would have been her first thought, not her last.

"I don't think so," she said, realizing it was true. "This whole experience has changed me. I think I might be interested in working in the emergency field, but not fighting fires. That's over for me. It would be tough for me to get cleared to work anyway, but that's not really the point. I want to be involved in another aspect—to be able to use what I've learned to help others who might be in the same spot."

"Well, I would have supported you either way, but I can't say I'm not relieved. What are you thinking about doing?"

Erin acknowledged what she wanted to do in a flash of her future that came to her as quickly as her past had, and her heart told her it was right.

"I'm going to retrain as a trauma counselor. Maybe get a degree and everything."

Kit seemed impressed. "That's terrific. I'm so proud of you—and I always have been, though I might not have acted like it. You'll be a great counselor—once you get your own head on straight, that is."

Erin laughed again, batting her sister's arm lightly. "Hey."

"You know what I mean. You need to resolve your own issues. Go talk to Bo, go face your fear. If he bows out, you'll survive it. You know you will. But at least you will have tried."

The thought of putting herself in a position to be rejected by Bo was a painful one, Erin thought, but her sister was right. And after all, that's what he had suffered from her. Maybe letting him walk away was the closure he needed.

"Okay. I will. I bet Hank's missing you. Maybe you should close and lock the door this time, or take it easy on the man. He's healing."

"And I love playing nurse," Kit said with a waggle of her eyebrows. Erin had to smile.

They hugged again, and Kit went back to Hank's room. Erin sat for a while longer, digesting everything Kit and Hank had said. She got up, left the hospital, and headed to Bo's apartment, where she knew he would be packing.

Getting ready to leave.

But not until they talked, she determined. Talked about everything.

14

Bo had no idea how he had accumulated so much stuff, but he had one day to deal with it, and so it had to be done.

He put things in corners of the room, the same way he would mentally separate evidence or parts of a crime scene. Books in one spot, tech in another, clothes all over the sofa. Pictures, dishes, kitchen implements, things from family and friends, other personal items all strewn in piles everywhere.

He hoped he had enough boxes. A truck rental waited for him the next morning, so he could pack this all up and drive it down to his new apartment in Virginia the day after. Then he'd fly back, get his car and a few last things.

One new life, to go.

There wouldn't be much time to unpack and settle in. He had a week before the task force was throwing him in the deep end, starting with some training on terrorism and biohazards. He had some experience with those things—he'd be getting more.

Welcome to the big leagues.

With a renewed spirit, he started grabbing boxes and stacks of bubble wrap and newspaper and got to work, thinking only about his packing and what was coming. Thinking about what he was leaving behind, well…that wasn't something he could do right now.

They'd solved the arsons, and though Erin's case remained open, he couldn't confront her about it. Maybe he couldn't confront the pain of knowing she would lie to him, keep things from him. His own fault.

He'd let himself believe something was different.

A knock on the door startled him. He didn't get a lot of unannounced visitors. Still, it could be a neighbor, or one of the guys from the station—a few folks had dropped by, hearing about his departure. He had a huge pan of lasagna in the fridge that had come in handy for dinners from the older lady down the hall as a goodbye gift.

"Just a second," he said, making a path to the door.

Erin was the last person he expected to see, making him suddenly feel as scattered as all of his belongings.

"Erin. What can I do for you?" he asked, sounding businesslike.

She pushed a hand through her hair, slightly longer now. She looked nervous, on edge. But she met his gaze steadily.

"Can I come in?"

He paused, and then stepped back to let her in.

"Sure. Don't mind the mess."

"You…you have a lot of stuff."

"Yeah, that's what I was thinking. I put a lot of things in drawers and closets over the years, I guess."

They both stood silently for a minute, hands in pockets.

"Listen, I know things are weird between us right now, but I think it's best if we just let things go. I have to get moving on this—is there a reason you came by?"

She flinched ever so slightly, and he regretted his tone, but then again, he didn't.

"I know you're busy getting ready for your move, but I needed to talk to you. To tell you some things, and…to ask your advice. About something delicate. And to apologize."

She said it all quick together, like trying to fit it all in. Bo blinked, unsure what to say. But his heart picked up rhythm, and he found himself nodding before he had consciously decided to, showing her to the only available chair at the island in the kitchen. He remained standing.

"Advice?" That was what he was most intrigued about, he supposed.

She swallowed visibly and clasped her hands in her lap.

"My memory came back—not one hundred percent, but most of it, I think. Definitely a lot more than before, big chunks, not just flashes."

In spite of the fact that he'd already guessed this, his eyebrows rose anyway. There was no doubt about the excitement in her voice, dim as it was.

He should tell her he knew, but he was curious where this was all going.

"I'm glad. When did this happen?"

"Um, the night of Hank's accident."

"I see."

"Yeah, well, and with it—well, I remember what happened at the fire. I know I should have come to you first, but I had to…take care of a loose end, and it's been tough to reconcile. I needed time to think, but honestly, thinking hasn't helped. The only person I knew who would know the right thing to do is you."

Bo felt as if the air had been knocked out of him.

"I'll do what I can," he offered noncommittally.

"Okay, here's what I know.…" She went on, telling him about the tape, the harassment. She was relatively unemotional about it, reporting it like news that had happened to someone else, until she got to the last part.

"So, in the warehouse, we were sent in to check for combustibles that they thought could be stored on the second floor. There weren't any. So that was good. That part of the warehouse wasn't on fire at that point, and when I turned to leave, to go back out and report to the chief, Joe grabbed me."

Her voice tightened, and she took a breath before continuing.

"The day before that fire, I'd told him I had the tape to make him stop bothering me. I thought it was the only way. When he grabbed me, he said that if I didn't tell him where the tape was, he'd make good and sure I never had a chance to use it. To make his point, he hit me. He told me how easy it would be to make sure I had an accident in a fire. That way, I'd never be able to report him."

Bo cursed on a whoosh of breath. Whatever he'd expected, he hadn't expected this. He wanted Joe alive so that he could beat the crap out of him. But she wasn't done yet.

"I hit him back—we fought, and that was why we both had some unusual bruises that the doctors couldn't explain. I ran, he chased me. I was going to tell the chief right then, or whoever would listen, and I had the bruises to prove it. Joe knew he'd made a big mistake, and he tackled me farther down on the first floor. It was unstable there, the fire having burned long enough to start on the supports around us. We struggled, and I managed to get to my feet." She swallowed hard again; this time she couldn't hold back her tears. "He shoved me down, hard. I think I hit my head, I don't know. Things got fuzzy. Then I heard him yell, and I heard the noise, knew something had gone terribly wrong. I looked over, saw the rafters coming down, saw Joe rolling, on fire. Screaming."

Bo reached for her hand, took it, squeezed. She was ice-cold.

"Erin, you don't have to say any more."

She took her hand from his.

"There isn't much more. I guess that's how he died. I only remember something large landing on me, too, pinning me, and the smoke choking me. Then, that's all. Until I woke up in the hospital, and I didn't know anything. I guess being at the hospital with the guys the other night, with Hank, hearing the machines, seeing his injuries… It brought it all rushing back. Or maybe it was the hypnotism, I don't know, but I really do remember now, and I have proof."

Bo's anger dissolved under his concern, and he pulled her against him whether she wanted it or not, wrapping his arms around her.

"I wish I could get a hold of him…" he said under his breath as she wept quietly into his chest.

"What happened was bad enough. But it was an accident, how he died, except for why we ended up there. I have the recording here in my bag," she said, sniffing as she slipped out of his embrace. "But to be honest, I almost destroyed it. I don't know what to do with it. So that's what I thought you could help me with."

"How so?"

"I can't see the point in bringing this to light. It would just hurt his family, be a smear on the department. But…it is the truth. And the truth is important, even if it is painful. Can I look myself in the mirror if I don't come forward with what I know? I keep going round and round, and yes, I should have come to you sooner, but it was… It's been a lot to process."

"And you had to do that alone," Bo said flatly. "As always. I always knew you were keeping something from me, back then—it was Joe. The harassment, wasn't it?"

She looked down, nodded again. "Yes. I know…believe me, it's been keeping me up nights that if I had just told you, if I had not been so prideful, thinking I could handle it, or worrying what everyone would think, then maybe he would be alive, and maybe none of this would have happened if I had acted otherwise."

"Some of that could be true, but what he did in that warehouse—everything he did—it was all on him. He got what he deserved, in my opinion, and the accident—that wasn't your fault. Don't take that on. But yes. You should have come to me. I wish you had."

"I know. I'm so, so sorry. Because it would have

been the smart thing to do, but also because, among everyone, you were the person I could trust. Should have trusted. I just… I don't know. I don't know entirely why it felt so critical that I handle everything myself, that I always had to be completely in control all the time."

The tightness in Bo's chest loosened as he listened as she continued.

"That's what scared me, too, I guess. My feelings for you, they weren't in my control. I loved you so much, and I guess I thought I was losing you when you moved up into investigation—so I pushed you away. I was also ashamed of what was happening with Joe, and he knew about us—he could have hurt your career prospects."

"No, he really couldn't have. That should have been the last of your concerns. And you weren't losing me. If you had only come to me, Erin—"

"I know. I shouldn't have waited until now. Apparently, I still have a few issues to work out, so Kit says," she shared on a short laugh. "This is all too late, but still, I wanted us to have…closure, I guess."

There was a peace in her face that Bo hadn't seen before—ever. As if all the poison had been let out. All the bad stuff she'd been holding in, she'd finally let go. And she'd shared it with him—maybe late, maybe not when he'd wished she had, but she had. She'd come to him, and now it was his turn.

She'd also said "loved"—past tense.

"Listen, you've been through so much. It would be enough to mess anyone up. But I think you're right about the recording. You should come forward. Joe's family has backed off any legal action, but there's always a threat of that. This would protect you. My advice would be to bring it to the new marshal, and I can go with you if you want. The case should be closed, and all the information should be there, including the recording. The physical evidence, the bruising, the progression of events, supports your story. It will be enough, I promise. Like you said, Joe's family deserves the truth, no matter how ugly, and the department can stand it. And this is something the department has to know, in case there were other victims."

"I never thought of that. I thought I was the only one."

He had to stop for a second, look away. The idea of anyone laying a hand on her—hitting her—made him so angry he almost couldn't contain it. But the fact that she'd also felt alone…it killed him to know that. Whatever responsibility she bore, he bore some, too, if she'd felt she couldn't be open with him.

"I'm sorry, Erin," he said, wishing he'd done things differently, too. That he hadn't let her go so easily. That he hadn't pushed or insisted that she share what was bothering her. Maybe he could have changed the outcome for the better—protecting her was part of his job, for crying out loud.

"I'd like it if you could come with me, but I understand if you can't," she said, glancing around at all of his scattered belongings. "I know you have to go."

"Of course I'll come. Whatever will help out."

Loved.

His heart was raw. Erin had admitted why she'd left him, why she'd held herself so distant. She'd apologized. This was what they'd hoped for—that she could remember, and that they could bring this all full circle.

It should have been the closure he was looking for, but nothing felt closed, except for maybe the case.

"While I'm being completely open, then, you know, the new me, and facing my fears and everything…" she said, breaking into his thoughts. Her voice was higher, a little thinner—still nervous.

"And?"

"I'm not going back to the job. I have something new, I think, that I want to do. This…all of what's happened, it changed me. I guess I thought when my memory returned, I would be the old me, with the old job, and old patterns—but I don't even want that."

"Or the old us."

"Yes, not that, either," she said.

"I get it. I'm grateful you're sharing—"

"But the new us…I want the new us. The us we were starting to be. I love you, but not how I loved you before…because that wasn't enough. If you're interested, I wondered…you know, considering that I nearly botched things up again, and that you're leaving, but if you'd want to…keep new us going?"

Bo sat down, his brain stuttering over the words she said, as if not hearing them correctly.

Love?

"You love me?"

"I do. So much. I love what we were becoming… but it was only a start, with me not remembering anything, and all that past behind us, all resolved, so I was hoping…" She paused, taking a breath, clasping her hands together again tightly in front of her, as if she had to hold on to *something*. "Anyway, I just wanted you to know how I felt, but if you—"

"I love you, too, Erin. I never stopped, but I like new us, too…it would be nice to see what we could be."

She beamed, and the shock in her eyes had him hauling her against him again, and this time he didn't want to let go. A fresh batch of tears soaked his shirt and she laughed as she cursed them. New Erin still hated crying—and that made him laugh, too.

Right now, he needed to kiss her and to make sure all of this was real. Finding her lips, he touched softly, then went deeper as her hands curled into his shoulders and she opened, tasting him as desperately as he was her.

Breathing more heavily, they parted, and Bo's mind reeled, his body hard, his heart light. Heady.

"The FBI job will be a challenge," he said, tipping his forehead against hers. "I might not be around even as much as I was with this one, but we'll make this work. I can come here, and we can figure out some kind of travel, stay in touch as much as we can. Something."

"Travel might not be necessary."

"Why's that?"

"I'm applying to Johns Hopkins in Baltimore for the fall. I want to get a psych degree and train as a trauma counselor. They have an amazing program, so I'm selling the house and moving down there. I already talked to a student adviser who knows the trauma counselor, Tom, who helped me. Tom's even giving me a recommendation. Maybe I can use what happened to me to assist other people in the same situation."

Bo grinned, and then he laughed. "That's wonderful."

"We should be able to find a place together, close

to the FBI office and school. I can commute…if you don't think it's too soon for that, I mean?"

"I think it's far past time, actually," he said.

As they talked, he'd worked his hands up under the back of her shirt, stroking the soft skin of her back.

Love. His.

"I have a few things to finish up here, though— selling the house and helping Kit save the store," she said, filling him in on Kit's financial difficulties. "I talked her into letting me hold some of the firefighter fund-raising events at her store—you know, like buy a bouquet, kiss a fireman kind of thing—to help her raise visibility, draw attention to her business."

"That's a good idea." Bo swooped in and began kissing her lips, her cheek.

"Oh," she said, catching her breath when he kissed her neck. "I thought so, too. She sent some lovely flower arrangements to Hank's room, and to the nurses' stations. The hospital gift shop clerk saw them—she was impressed, and talked to Kit about possibly being the supplier for the hospital florist. It would be a huge account for her."

"That's also a good idea," Bo murmured against her skin, starting to work the snap of her jeans. "I love you," he said against her mouth. "Who you were, who you are…who you're going to be. All of you."

She looked up at him with a sweet-hot gaze so full of emotion that it humbled him. How could he ever have thought he could live without her?

"I love you, too. I'll never hold anything back again. We're in this together. I promise."

"I like the sound of that," he said, caressing her.

"Shouldn't we work on packing up all this stuff? I could help."

"It can wait," he said, his lips raining kisses down from her throat to her breast, making her gasp.

"You're sure?"

Her expression held all the love and promise Bo had ever imagined, and he smiled. He felt his heart expand at the thought of the future they were going to have together.

"Absolutely sure. We have plenty of time. The rest of our lives, in fact."

* * * * *